To Carolyn
Thankyou!

A.W.

TOO LATE?

TOO LATE?
Copyright © A. W. Jackson (2024)
The right of A.W. Jackson to be identified as the author of this work has been asserted by them in accordance with section 77 and 78 of the Copyright, Designs and Patents Act 1988.

All rights reserved.

No part of this publication may be reproduced, stored in a retrieval system, or transmitted in any form or by any means, electronic, mechanical, photocopying, recording, or otherwise, without the prior written permission of the author. Any person who commits any unauthorised act in relation to this publication may be liable to criminal prosecution and civil claims for damages.

This book is a work of fiction. Names, characters, places and incidents are either products of the author's imagination or are used fictitiously. Any resemblance to any events, locales, or persons, living or dead, is entirely coincidental.

ISBN 9798326842121 (Paperback)

https://www.awjackson.co.uk

A NOVELLA

BY A. W. JACKSON

A NOTE FROM THE AUTHOR

I have always struggled with my mental health and often times those issues have entangled themselves with the fact that I am a queer person. I am lucky enough that I have supportive friends and family who have helped me through the worst days and without whom I may not be here writing this book. Some members of our community, however, aren't so lucky, and often need someone to talk to. Thus, as a small way of paying back to our community, I will be donating 25% of the royalties earned from this book to the charity Switchboard:

Switchboard is the national LGBTQIA+ support line. For 50 years, their volunteers, who identify as LGBTQIA+, have been available to discuss anything related to sexuality and gender identity; whether it's sexual health, relationships or just the way you're feeling. Switchboard's support line is completely free, and available wherever you feel most comfortable – whether that's on the phone, via chat or email. 10am-10pm every single day.

If you feel affected by the topics in this story, then please visit Switchboard's website printed below to take the next steps in finding help. Alternatively, you can call their hotline, also printed below.

https://switchboard.lgbt
0800 0119 100

CHAPTER 1

WHAT'S THE POINT?

Here I find myself, once again, staring into the abyss that is the collection of pill bottles laid out on my bedside table. The concoction of medicines would surely be enough to kill an elephant and, although I am fat, I would like to think that I'm not quite on par with an elephant just yet. Thus, the pills must surely be enough to kill me, too.

I can't express how tempting it is to just pop each cap, chug them all, and wash them down with a glass of rosé. But that won't happen, because I can tell you right now exactly how this is going to play out. It's the same every time.

I'll stare deeply at the pick 'n' mix of pills; some chalky, others deliciously sugar-coated. I'll probably *keep* staring at them for a good hour. I'll voice all the reasons why I hate myself, and why I should just end it – my life, if you're not following – to my otherwise empty, shitty little apartment.

Then, when I've tortured myself to the point where the words no longer mean anything, I'll start the cutting. When *that* no longer brings any pain, or even a tear to my eye, I'll sit there and finally contemplate downing all the technicoloured candy-like tablets.

That's when the tiny, sensical part of my brain will kick in and convince me that I'm too much a of a chicken to go through with it. At which point, I'll place all the bottles back into my mirror cabinet above the sink in my bathroom, and I'll numbly fall asleep in preparation for another day of the hell on earth that is my life.

Before we see what tomorrow brings, I understand that I've been rather rude and not given you any context as to who I am and how I got to this place. So, here's a little 'previously on' montage for you, as if you've started watching a show from season three.

I'm Brian, by the way. You probably deserve to know that, considering you're about to go on this crazy journey with me. I'm twenty-three and I work in a bank in Manhattan, but more on that later.

I have short, mousey-brown hair, and blue eyes. I *used* to have a visible jawline, and I have a slightly turned-up nose that hopefully I've grown into. I'm also six-foot and a bottom twink – not a combination that is super fun when your ideal man is supposed to be taller than you.

TOO LATE?

I guess the beginning of all my woes really started with my parents. You see, back in high school, I was a late bloomer. I was the last one to grow hair *down there* and the last to have their voice break – though I'm still convinced that it never did. If you're imagining what it sounds like right now, then picture Mickey Mouse with a slight Texan country twang.

I blame my dodgy voice on the fact that my Adam's apple is wonky and off-centre. That excuse used to work when I was still a short, skinny twink in high school and you could actually *see* my Adam's apple. These days, I'm a giant, and there's a lovely rubber ring of flab around my neck covering my Adam's apple, so there's no proving it. The blubber now covers most of my body and I hate it. No matter how many pitying exes try to tell me I'm beautiful, I'm quite confident that I'll never believe it.

Any who, back to being a late bloomer, and all. One thing that certainly did not hit me later in life was that I AM GAY. If my obsession with Justin Russo from *Wizards of Waverly Place* wasn't enough to alert me, the second I saw some of the more mature boys in the locker room sporting hairy, puffed-out chests, and deeper voices, I knew for sure that I was born to suck dick.

There was, and is, no two ways about it. The only thing I see in a girl is a potential bestie. Someone I can sit and watch *RuPaul's Drag Race* with. Someone to judge the beautiful and talented competitors with as we sprawl across a sofa eating chips, delusionally thinking we're Tyra Banks.

Anyway, sorry, we were once again on a tangent. Although, if I'm being honest, you should probably prepare yourself for a lot of these, because I'm not changing for anybody – even if you did buy this book.

So, though I knew I was gay from a young age, I also knew that my parents were religious, redneck Texans and so, coming out wasn't really an option. Now, don't get me wrong, I know that not all religious Americans are homophobes, but my mum and her Church most definitely are.

I kept my secret just that – a secret – and only told my bestie at the time, Rachel. Her and, of course, all of the cute jocks I hooked up with, who were also closeted. Though, the difference between me and them, was that they were closeted because they themselves hadn't accepted the fact that they were gay yet.

They were the kind of 'straight boys' who say things like:

"I'm not gay, guys are just better at sucking dick," or,

"It's not gay unless we do anal," or – and this is my personal favourite –

"I'm just practicing for when I really lose my virginity to *insert random redneck girl name like 'Tammy' here*."

Oh, so you didn't lose your virginity the last three times we had sex then? I'd keep that thought to myself rather than say it out loud. You see, they were still big, dangerous, and touchy enough, that if I kicked up a fuss, they'd probably beat me up.

Also, I do need to mention that the Texan twang is only slight because I worked very hard to rid myself of that silly accent. Instead, I adopted a plainer standard-American accent. It stems, for the most part, through

TOO LATE?

watching Disney Channel and Nickelodeon which, on reflection, I'm surprised my parents even let me watch.

My parents were always suspicious of my sexuality but, luckily, Rachel agreed to be my beard. She became my girlfriend – to satisfy my Bible-bashing, racist, and homophobic parents. And I became her boyfriend – so that her mother didn't have to worry about some beefy jock knocking up her only daughter. But although I might've been passing as straight, there was no doubt in anyone's mind that I could ever be some hound dog looking to get his dick wet.

Everything was going well, for a while, and our parents were fooled. I got to keep on hooking up with guys, and so did Rachel. That was until my so-called 'best friend,' and I had a falling out over something so dumb that, even to this day, I still can't remember what it was. But maybe that's because it was massively overshadowed by what happened next.

Long story short, in a truly spiteful act of bratty rage, Rachel outed me to my parents. I never spoke to her again, let alone forgave her. Shit hit the fan, to say the least. I returned home that day to see my parents arguing in the kitchen. They spotted me out of the corner of their eyes and, in tandem, marched up to me to confront me about my devilish 'life choices.'

My father is a tall, bald, muscular figure of a man who owns a local hardware store. We'd never been that close but, up until that point, we'd had an unspoken type of communication with each other. It was weird, but it worked. It usually consisted of side-eyes, smirks, and grunts at my mother's expense. My mother is a short, busty, blonde lady who loves Jesus more than anything in the world, especially me. Again, we were never that close, but she is my mom and, at the time, she was decent enough.

I'd never seen my mom look so angry, apart from whenever she saw a human of a race other than hers – I mentioned they're racist, right? She was practically foaming at the mouth, and though my father wasn't quite as intimidating, he wasn't doing anything to calm the situation, either.

"Is it true?" she asked, scowling at me as if I were a stranger.

"That I'm gay? Yes. That I'm some kind of devil-worshipping sicko? No," I answered, standing my ground.

"Well then, you're no son of mine," she said with ease. I caught my father's eye glance to her in shock before turning back to me, his eyes now glossy as if he were about to shed a tear. Before I could utter another word, my mother kicked me out there and then. She threw a gym bag at me, and told me to fill it and go. My dad just watched as she seemingly made the decision for both of them. The decision to never see or speak to me again.

In theory, I should've been happy that I didn't have to hide who I was anymore. Happy that I wouldn't have to live under her evil rule. But, even if your mom's a stone-cold piece of shit, she's still your mom and, experiencing what I did, it broke me.

I was eighteen, a high school dropout, and homeless. With nothing but a bag full of clothes, my phone, and a wallet with some cash that I'd saved from birthdays and Christmases, I headed to New York on a

TOO LATE?

whim and never looked back. Although, that's not completely true. Every night, I send my dad a text to say goodnight and, of all the one thousand, eight hundred, and twenty-five times that I've sent it thus far, I've still never been gifted a response. There's some idiotic part of me, though, that feels like if I keep trying, one day he'll see sense and remember who I am to him.

After a year of living in Brooklyn, I'd somehow managed to secure a job and apartment – albeit a shitty apartment, in a neighbourhood full of crackheads, but it was *my* shitty apartment. I even got a pet dog named Copper. Although things were definitely improving, a lot of damage had been done, and the shunning of myself by my entire family really took a toll on me.

I binge-ate all the time from the stress and depression, until I became twice the twink I once was. Despite that, one man *did* take interest in me – Ben. He was about my height, had long blond hair and green eyes. He wasn't my usual type, but he *was* hot and, most importantly, he was gay and – out! Most of the men I'd hooked up with on Grindr, up until that point, had been just the same as the jocks back in high school. 'Masc. discreet,' is the term they use, I believe.

The first few years together were bliss. The sex was great, he was great, and he had a good job – some high-end corporate job that never really made any sense when he tried to explain it. Copper even loved him, which said a lot because that dog was grumpy towards me most days.

As time went on, though, I found it harder and harder not to feel inadequate. He went to the gym five days a week and looked like a Greek god, and I suppose the novelty of being with a chubbier guy wore off for him, as he became distant to the point where we hardly ever touched one another.

How was I *not* supposed to feel inadequate? We'd watch *Mean Girls* for the thousandth time – deservedly so, what a pop culture moment, right? – and whilst I was balancing a bowl of chips on my stomach, he'd be sat there on his phone, snacking on a plain rice cake. Who does that?

I told him about my feelings, how fat and ugly I felt, and his reply to that was always the same.

"No, you're not."

Very inspired.

It also *really* didn't help my self-esteem that, whenever we went out, all the twinks within a three-mile radius would sniff him out. They'd ogle at him, giving me dirty looks, and I always knew what that look meant. It was the, 'how are they a couple?' look. It also wound me up to see the glint in his eye as they fawned over him. It was obvious he was enjoying it a little too much.

In the end, I was right. He eventually found his balls and dumped me like he had so clearly wanted to do for a long time. He *said* he was dumping me because of my constant insecurities, and that he was sick of having to try and make me feel better. He *said* that it was all in my head, and that I was crazy, before ironically *then* adding that he'd been banging some little twig from his gym for several months.

"So, I was right!" I shouted, glaring at him.

"Whatever, Brian. I don't care who was right. The point is, it's over. *We're* over!" he said with an unnecessarily patronising tone to his voice. "Oh, and I'm taking Copper with me," he added with nonchalance.

TOO LATE?

"Like hell you are!" The audacity of the man, to think that he could call me crazy, cheat on me, and then steal *my* dog! "Copper can decide for himself," I blurted out, feeling sure of myself.

We placed Copper in the middle of us, and called out to him until he chose a side – and choose a side he certainly did. But he chose the wrong one. The rotten mutt sided with him. To be honest though, that only confirmed the theory in my mind that he'd been letting Copper lick peanut butter off his balls. Rather him than me, anyway. So, off they went, leaving me alone with nothing but my shitty job that I really hate, low self-esteem, and a plethora of mental health issues.

Now then, what's this infamous job, I hear you pondering? Well, you already know that I work in a bank, but it's not just *any* bank. ABA bank is the kind of bank that rich people use, which means that the majority of the customers are . . . how do you say . . . oh yeah – dicks!

Though, even amongst the richest Manhattanites, there is still a hierarchy. You have the true VIP customers that the upstairs-workers deal with, and then the elite wannabes that aren't quite rich enough to own a skyscraper yet. Those are the ones who we, on the ground floor, deal with behind our little Plexiglas counters.

Don't get me wrong, there *are* some nice customers, but they are greatly outweighed by the bad ones. The bad ones who are rude, blunt and, for some bizarre reason, think that I, someone who works behind a desk, am to blame when the interest rates fluctuate out of their favour. Oh, how they love to display such disparaging thoughts to me on a daily basis.

If you haven't caught on to this by now, then let me make it clear – I hate the majority of people. Most people are impatient, annoying, and stupid bags of flesh, that only seem to make my life worse, which I really don't need. It especially doesn't help when my social anxiety is poked and prodded at on a daily basis by wealthy middle-aged men in New York. If that weren't bad enough, whenever I'm having a particularly dark and depressing episode, and am in need of a mental health day, it falls upon the deafest ears the world can seem to find – my boss.

Susan, is her name, and I guess being a heartless bitch is her game. You see, Susan doesn't *understand* mental health, but instead of being an open-minded member of society, who realises that just because she doesn't have it, doesn't mean it's not real, she instead takes the approach that it's all made up. She believes that all of us *crazy* people conspired together to create mental illness because we're too lazy to work. It's ironic really, because carrying out her conspiracy theory sounds like it would entail far more work than me actually showing up for my shift.

Susan is one of the aforementioned dumb, annoying, and impatient humans, and I hate her. I will be truly disappointed if I succeed in killing myself before I have the luxury of watching her go first. She's in her fifties now, anyway, so she's more than halfway there, I guess.

Now then, it's time to move on to the only person in the world who gives me any scrap of hope – Carmen. She is a sexy, bisexual Latina with long, thick, black locks, perfectly slicked-back baby hairs and deliciously hazel

TOO LATE?

eyes. Maybe she likes hanging around with me because my ugly mug makes her look even more beautiful. She's my best friend, but also my only friend. I'm not one hundred percent sure where I fall on *her* best friend list because, well, she's not a complete loner like me. But I'm okay not knowing, because she's a great best friend to me.

We work together, watch *Drag Race* together, and we used to go 'out out' a lot together, but I haven't been on a night out with Carmen since the whole breakup I told you about earlier. Even though she's amazing and loves me, and I'm sure she actually *would* miss me if I were to go, she still doesn't know the full story of who I am. Of course, she knows about the less-than-ideal mental health situation, but she doesn't know how bad it's gotten. So far, only you know that.

How do you tell someone that you spend most nights trapped in a vicious cycle of directing pain and hatred into the reflection of your bathroom mirror? I don't know what my poor reflection ever did to me, it's not like it's *him* making my life decisions. Besides, reflections are literally the opposite of what you look like, and when you have an asymmetrical face like mine, it's an even *more* twisted version of reality staring back at you. It's so strange that you hardly ever see the real you.

I'm fully aware that my left eye is almost a full centimetre lower than my right, but my reflection understands what is needed and, thus, lies to me, telling me that they're perfectly level. So, even though my reflection isn't me, I definitely prefer it. It lies to me to make me feel better and it takes all the shit I throw at it without answering back.

Anyway, I'm off on another tangent. The point is, I hate my life.

I have no family, no furry companion, and my only friend still doesn't know that I'm in a constant state of teetering on the edge of a cliff – metaphorically, and sometimes literally. I know Carmen cares. I can see it in her eyes when she pities me, but she doesn't know what to say, and who can blame her? It's not like you get taught in school how to ask someone if they're suicidal. Equally, there are no lessons on how to *tell* your friend that you're suicidal. I wouldn't know what to say to me, either, if I was in her shoes.

My therapist seems to think she knows what to say to me but, in all honesty, I'm yet to see a decent return on my one hundred and fifty dollars an hour where she's concerned. Yep, you heard right, one hundred and fifty. It's like they want me to be mentally ill *and* poor. Also, sorry, I forgot to mention that my therapist knows about the kooky thoughts too, so you're actually number two.

Finally, you're all caught up. Now we can get back to me staring at my pills where, right on schedule, the tiny, reasonable part of my brain wakes up, sees the pills, and reminds me that I am, indeed, too weak to perform such a task as to kill myself today. And so, I put the pills back into the cabinet and I go to bed, where I prepare myself for another mundane day of my hateful life.

CHAPTER 2

THE EASY WAY OUT

I wake up to the incessant chiming sound of my alarm clock. Still half asleep, I flap my arm about the bedside table in the hopes that one of my fingers will land on the smallest button in the world to disarm the evil device. Thankfully, it does.

I wipe the sleep from my eyes and roll out of bed, before dragging myself to the shower. I sing my little heart out to *Fantasy* by Mariah Carey, which for years I thought said "sweet, sweet medicine baby." Trust me, you'll hear it next time you listen. During my Superbowl shower-time performance I'm simultaneously fantasising about new and inventive ways to off myself that I could implement on my way to work. Not that I'll ever use them. Even though I know I'll never have the guts to go through with it, it doesn't detract from how it feels just to *have* such thoughts. It's like you're a worthless piece of garbage that should be incinerated, but the conveyor belt delivering you to the incinerator keeps breaking down just before you get there.

What really cheeses me off, is when people come out with particularly dumb shit like:

"Don't be so down in the dumps," or,

"Think positively," or,

"Do things that make you happy," and, finally,

"You should drink more water; it completely changes your outlook on life."

Where do these people get off? I'd *love* to be happy, positive and drink water like a god damn goldfish, but it isn't that easy. What people don't understand about depression and anxiety is that they can consume you. It's certainly not a tap that you can turn on and off. I can't just *decide* to have a happy day.

I don't control it; it controls me.

If I'm lucky enough to have a good day, then great, but don't be mistaken. That's one day out of three hundred and sixty-five, and that doesn't mean I'm better. It means I got lucky that day, and chances are that the next one will be back to normal which, in my case, means crap. Telling someone who has mental health issues the above things, is like telling someone in surgery to just "relax and not think about it," while a surgeon is elbow deep inside them rearranging their organs. At least surgery patients usually get put to sleep. I have to be conscious through my suffering.

TOO LATE?

After my shower, I dry myself off and grab my dull, grey uniform. I slip into it or, more accurately, I shimmy my fat ass into my work trousers that, for some reason, only come in slim fit. As I do up my last shirt button, hoping that it doesn't ping off, I flick the tv on, looking for a distraction from the fact that in sixty short minutes time, I'll be in work. The news pops onto the screen and it looks somewhat interesting, so I turn it up as I head to the kitchen for some cereal.

"Yep, that's right! Texan preacher, Andy Waterson, has just been accused of several accounts of sexual assault on minors!" I hear the onsite reporter say to her counterparts back in the studio, and I pop my head around the kitchen door to catch a glimpse of the creep.

It's crazy how people think it's us LGBTQ+ folk, with our drag queens and non-binary humans, that are the danger to children. When, in reality, there's a paedophile lurking around every altar. I mean, once or twice is a coincidence, but so far this year, that's the tenth religious figure caught for being 'inappropriate' with kids, and a whole zero drag queens. Insert eyeroll here.

I finish my cereal and tip the bowl to my mouth to slurp the sugary leftover milk –because, if we're being honest with ourselves, it's the only reason any of us actually eat cereal. I leave the bowl next to the mountain of pots building up beside my sink, that I swear I'll get to at some point.

As I'm getting ready to leave my dump of an apartment and head to work, I realise that I can't find my phone. I search through the trash and, as I'm doing so, come to the realisation that one of the few things that keeps me alive, is the fear of someone finding my body in the pit that is my apartment. I'd be all over the news and not for the right reasons. If I'm ever on the news, it should be because someone overheard my insane Mariah Carey karaoke cover in my shower, not because they found me half naked, having choked to death on a cheese puff.

I swear I haven't always been such a slothful pig when it comes to cleaning. It's only since *he* left, that I've been slacking around the house. *But*, I'm totally over him now, and ready to clean up!

Maybe.

I mean, it's now been like two or three months. Okay, four months two weeks and three-and-a-half days. But really, who's counting? Anyway, where the fuck is my – oh, found it! It's sticking out from under my bed where I must've kicked it under this morning. I pick the phone up and squeeze the power button with my finger. It flashes on for a singular moment to tell me that I have one measly percent of battery.

"Fuck!" I scream.

I have no time to charge it, and so now I need to bring my charger with me to work. I know that doesn't sound so bad but, to me, it's just another thing that my fat, dumb ass messed up. Why can't I even successfully charge a phone, for crying out loud?

I grab my bag and leave my dumpy apartment, heading to work on my bike. And no, it's not a motor bike. I am neither cool nor brave enough to have one of those. Though, by no means do I ride a bicycle by choice. I have a driver's license but, unfortunately, I can't afford a car, and we've already established that I hate people, so I'm

TOO LATE?

sure you can see why I wouldn't ever contemplate taking public transport.

One thing that really winds me up, though, is that even though I've been riding to work for the past few months, I've lost like, one whole pound in weight. Sure, I eat about four thousand calories a day, but I really don't see how that's got anything to do with it. I even get my five a day in there too – *strawberry* doughnuts, *banana* milkshake, and even Fanta – so who is anyone to tell me about a well-balanced diet?

I ride along, minding my own business, being as courteous as I can to drivers because, from my driving days, I remember just how annoying some cyclists can be. If only the drivers were as equally courteous back. Case in point being the turd-on-wheels behind me who keeps trying to overtake when there's clearly no room and a heap of oncoming traffic. If he could just be patient for ten more seconds, he would see that, up ahead, the road widens once more. Instead of honking consistently.

He continues his little show as he swerves in a bid to try, I assume, and intimidate me. But what he doesn't know, is that I am indifferent to whether I survive this encounter or not, so his intimidation attempts are futile. He adds some more honking of his horn to further dramatize the situation, but I just flip him the bird and carry on pedalling at the fastest pace my chubby thighs can handle without chafing. Before now, I've had days where sparks have practically flown out from between my thighs.

Inevitably, the idiot decides to overtake, knocking me over as he speeds off. The cars behind him pretend not to have seen my predicament as they drive by, one after another. But hey, it's NYC! Everyone's got somewhere to be, right? Yes! And that includes me.

I dust myself off, and drag my bike to the sidewalk, noticing the rip in the knee of my trousers, and the bit of scraped, fleshy skin hiding beneath it. *Gross.* I do that thing where you touch something that you know is going to hurt, but still do it anyway, just to be sure.

Can't wait to get a drilling from Susan for this.

I internalise my anger, as I'm surrounded by people, and I need to pretend to be fine so that some fake do-gooder doesn't try to talk to me to make themselves feel better. Annoyingly, it's too late to turn back for another pair of trousers, and I can't even call ahead to tell them I'm going to be late, because my phone isn't charged.

The guy that ran me down could've at least done me a favour and finished the job, putting me out of my miserable existence. Alas, I'm still here, and now I must walk my bike to work as the incident has also bent one of my wheels out of shape.

Forty minutes later, I arrive at ABA Bank. It stands for American Banking Associates but, if you ask me, I think the CEO is a closeted gay who wanted to sneak in an ABBA reference. I'm a little late, but I believe that's justified, all things considered. Of course, Susan won't see it that way, and she collars me the second I walk in.

"What time do you call this?" she asks, in her usual patronising voice.

"Ten past nine," I utter back, internally eyerolling as I prepare for the pointless back-and-forth.

"And what time are you supposed to start work?" She continues her interrogation by folding her arms.

"Nine, but I got hit by a car on the way," I explain.

TOO LATE?

"And that makes you late, does it?" she asks with a raised eyebrow that makes me want to punch her.

"Er . . . yeah bec–" I try to reason with her, but I am cut off.

"And why is your uniform ripped? This is unacceptable," she says, looking down at my bloodied knee.

Is she seriously this brain-dead?

"Well, I was hit–" She cuts me off once again.

"No, no, I don't have time for excuses. Just get yourself behind your counter and get to work!"

I slap a fake smile across my face and do as she says, praying that *she* gets hit by a truck on her way home tonight. ABA Bank wouldn't be caught dead with a bike shed outside, far too common for their clientele, so I stick my bike in the staffroom like I always do. Propped up against Susan's locker just to piss her off. I head to my counter where I'll stand for the next eight hours, hating my life, while people with much more money than myself moan about how they still don't have enough and create reasons for it to be my fault. Luckily, I'm next to Carmen today, so that should make the time pass sooner.

"Hi," she says as she notices me park myself in the counter booth beside her.

"Hey," I smile genuinely, which is a rare thing these days.

"How are you?" she asks, making me wonder whether or not I should tell her about last night, or *every* night, for that matter.

"Been better," I say instead.

"Having a bad day?" she asks, with a sincere look of concern.

"You could say so," I reply, playing into the pity party as I flash her my fleshy knee.

"Oh my god, what happened?" she gasps.

"I got hit by some idiot in a Porsche on the way in."

"Jesus! Are you all right?" Carmen's face widens in shock and confusion. She's probably wondering why I still bothered to show up. After all, I hate it here, and usually I'd use any excuse not to come in. But, in all honesty, I thought it might be good for me to see a friendly face. It was either that, or go back home and spend all day staring at my pill collection and, well, you know what happens when I do that.

"Yeah, I'm fine, it's just a scratch," I say exposing her to my knee again causing her to visibly gag. "So, anything new with you?" I ask, in the hopes she has something exciting going on that I can live through vicariously.

"Well, I didn't get hit by a car on the way to work but, I *did* get some action last night," she smirks.

"Ooh, tell me everything. Boy, girl?" I plea.

"Boy."

See, I told you Carmen would have something fun going on. Besides, it's been far too long since I've seen a dick that isn't either mine, or an eleven-incher from a porn video.

"Brian, he was *so* hot – and your type, too!"

"What, breathing?" I joke.

"Shut up, you know what I mean," she laughs. "You're into tall, dark, handsome and a little hairy," she smiles with one eyebrow raised.

"Okay, fair, that is definitely my type. So, what happened?"

TOO LATE?

"Well, he–" she started before being rudely cut off by someone who wanted serving.

"Tell me the rest later," I whisper, as she gets an earful from a customer. At least now I have some gossip to look forward to over lunch.

Fuck my life, I think to myself as I see Mr Fredrickson walk over to my counter.

"Hi, Mr Fredrickson," I feign sincerity in the hopes that in the last twenty-four hours he's become less of an entitled jerk. He's one of the mediocre rich ones that I told you about before, and the kind of person who wears sunglasses inside, which is weird enough as it is, but even more so when it's overcast *outside*.

"Hello, Brian," he replies with surprising politeness. This is followed by meaningless chatter that I don't register. I tend to tune him out these days, as he always comes in for the same thing, so I don't see any reason why today would be any different. I pull up his account on my screen and withdraw five grand from his account with a statement, before turning back to hear him ask for exactly that. You see, he's one of these old cronies that doesn't believe in paying by card, which is ridiculous, but he seems to make it work. That, or he's money laundering for a cartel. God, I wish it was that. At least that would be interesting.

"Here you are, already done it for you," I say with a smile.

"Oh, that was quick," he says with what looks like a frown, though it's hard to tell when he's still wearing his sunglasses. So much can be said with eyes. Love, hate, happy, sad. Is he sad? He seems sad. But why would he be sad? Okay now the word 'sad' is starting to lose its meaning. Did he *not* want me to be efficient? He doesn't have a problem complaining when I'm not fast enough. I just don't get people.

"Anything else?" I offer, to try and coax him out of this awkward silence.

"No, that'll be all. See you tomorrow," he answers, his face stern once more, disguising any vulnerability on show.

"Er . . . yeah, bye." Well, that was weird. Though I suppose no weirder than normal in the grand scheme of things.

An hour or so later and there's a massive queue. Carmen and I give each other a look of dread, but also support, as we simultaneously call over the next customers. Before they can reach our counters, the front doors fly open, and the rippling sound of gunshots echo about the lobby. The firing shots hit the ceiling's chandelier, dropping it to the ground, and causing shards of glass to scatter across the marble floor. Everyone ducks in a knee jerk reaction, me included, and then as we all slowly arise, the culprits make themselves known.

"Everybody, get down now!" the two of them shout frantically, firing another shot into the air. Everyone begins doing as they say including the two security guards, who don't bother trying to play hero as they dive to the floor and onto their stomachs. For some reason, I'm still stood up, making me stick out like a sore thumb amongst the sea of petrified, crying bodies.

Carmen is on the floor beside me, hidden from them by the counter, and she's calling my name, begging me to duck under with her. But . . . what's the point? Last night, I was ready to end my life but I chickened out. *Now,*

TOO LATE?

I have the perfect solution! I can die without having to get my own hands dirty! Carmen's calls become more like whispers as the two masked infiltrators walk closer, crunching the broken glass beneath their boots.

"Hey, you! Get down, now!" They both turn their guns towards me. I'm no gun expert but I'd assume they're some kind of semi-automatic rifle the way they were firing them off. I'm pretty sure my dad would know if he were here. He loved taking me to the shooting range, I merely entertained it for his sake. Oh right, not a good time to be on another tangent.

Staring down one of the barrels, I calmly and quietly reply, "No."

They turn and glare at each other, each gesturing for the other to take the lead. They clearly didn't expect much friction against their plan. It is silently decided that the one who is already closest to me will carry on being 'in charge' of the situation. Though, by the looks of it, these newbs weren't 'in charge' of anything. The 'boss' keeps their gun uncomfortably close to my face while the other nameless criminal turns their weapon to the crowd of people on the ground in a bid to keep them there.

"Fine, you can be the one to open the registers and fill this," they say throwing me a stained pillowcase. Also, notice how I say *they* because I don't know their gender. Not so hard, is it?

"No," I say calmly, throwing that gross pillowcase back at them.

"What the fuck is wrong with you?" they begin to moan.

Too much to go into detail about now.

"Are you fucking stupid? Do it, now! Or I'll blow your fucking brains out!" they say, coming so close to my face that even through the balaclava I can smell the coffee on their breath.

"Kill me. I want to die," I whisper back, only loud enough for the coffee-breathed human to hear. They're clearly stunned and confused, but also angry that I'm not doing as I'm told. They keep their finger teasing the trigger as the gun continues to be planted firmly in front of my face, with only the Plexiglas between us.

Now, it's *my* patience that begins to run out, as they either need to kill me and get this done with, or they need to leave. Lunch starts in ten minutes and, you better believe, If I'm to continue suffering this existence, then I won't be made late for my favourite time of the day – which is anytime that I eat, really.

"Come on then! If you're going to shoot me, then shoot me already!" I shout loud enough that everyone in the room can hear.

Their hand tenses up on the trigger, and I close my eyes happily, ready to leave my physical body behind and enter whatever it is that comes after, because it can't be worse than this. Though, I won't lie, the anticipation of waiting for it to –

CHAPTER 3

A HERO?

My closed eyelids squint and flutter as I hear the sound of a bullet being fired. Death, so far, doesn't feel too bad, and I don't seem to be in any pain at all. I can't even feel where the bullet hit me. Just as I await my guiding light to show up and lead me down the path to the afterlife, I hear Carmen's voice whispering to me. God, I hope she isn't dead too, she actually enjoyed her life. Her whispers grow in volume.

"Brian, what are you doing?"

My eyes open to see, to my disappointment, that I'm still in the land of the living. The gun is still in front of me, but I could swear it went off? That's when I notice that the Plexiglas screen between us is cracked, and does indeed have a bullet hole in it. The hole a few inches to the right of my face.

"That was your warning shot!" they say, once again thinking that they have some hold over me. They really aren't understanding what I want out of the situation.

"No, this is *your* warning," I begin, getting a little closer to the screen to add, "next time, don't miss."

"Would you just fuck off, you psycho! I don't want to shoot anybody!"

"Then stop wasting my time and leave."

Jeez, these really are amateurs.

"Come on, let's just go! We're taking too long and they've probably already set off an alarm!" the clearly smarter of the two says.

I look down at my personal alarm button under the counter for the first time today. Truth be told, I had completely forgotten about it. I *would've* pressed it if I hadn't been so caught up in the moment – I'm not *totally* selfish. Just because I saw my way out of here, doesn't mean I wouldn't have alerted the police to save the others. I just . . . forgot. Glancing to my left, I see that Carmen has already pressed her button, as there's a little flashing blue light above it, indicating the police are on their way.

The person whose gun is still waving around in my face, is becoming even more erratic than before. They're frustrated – which I understand, as I've been told that I can be quite a pain in the ass – and they seem to be ignoring their friend's pleas to leave. Instead, they look directly at me with growing anger, eyes in the holes of their balaclava squinting. They might actually have what it takes to shoot me this time.

TOO LATE?

Just as they look like they're about to line up another shot, this time between my eyes, sirens ripple through the room. Their accomplice screams at them to leave and, finally, they comply, both gun-wielders running out of the front door. The sound of sirens grows louder, and tyres screech as the cops pull up to the building just in time to stop them from making a quick getaway. Even though I didn't get what I wanted out of that interaction, it worked out rather luckily for everyone else, as I seemed to stall the attackers long enough for the police to arrive.

"Brian! I don't know how the fuck you did that, but it was incredible!" Carmen pipes up as she finally lifts herself off the floor.

"Did what?" I ask, lending her my hand to help her up.

Before Carmen can answer me, all of the other customers and staff begin clapping.

"Wow! That was amazing!" one person shouts.

"Brian! I didn't know you had it in you!" a security guard says.

"What a hero!" someone I've never seen before calls out.

I'm being showered with compliments and applause by everyone, which is crazy enough, but then something happens that *really* makes me think that the world's gone mad.

"Brian, that wasn't the worst thing you've ever done," Susan says, which is the highest compliment I've ever heard the witch give.

"Er . . . thanks everyone," I utter, my brain trying to make sense of this strange feeling. In response, the applause loudens, and everyone is smiling at me as if I'm their saviour. In reality, I just wanted a one-way ticket out of here.

The police barge in, telling everyone to put their hands in the air as they check for any more perpetrators, thus bringing the awkward celebratory moment to an end. Once the officers do their sweep and clear the building, we all get checked over by medics before being sent home. I have a little ringing in my ear from the bullet-firing, but other than that, I'm fine. A few others got some scratches from the broken glass but, all in all, it seems everyone got away pretty unscathed.

Upon returning home, I get a call from the bank to say that we're all getting a paid week off for our trauma. They're closing for a few days anyway, for repairs, then staff from another branch will cover the remaining few days after that. The paid time off is most definitely welcome, even if I'm strangely not that traumatised. To be honest, I think I'm more unnerved by the fact that Susan practically loves me now. Also, respect to the poor souls they got to cover us from another branch. I wouldn't, if I were them.

The next morning, I wake to a knocking on my apartment front door. I'm not expecting anybody, and I still have morning breath, so let's hope that this isn't the day where my dream of a hunky man showing up at my door, is finally answered. The knocking continues in rushed bursts, without so much as a second's respite between them. Who could possibly need to see me this urgently on a Tuesday morning? I clamber out of bed, and move close enough to the door so that I can shout, "who is it?"

TOO LATE?

"It's me," Carmen's voice answers through the door. "You've got to let me in, you won't believe what's happening!"

"Okay," I sigh.

I open the door to reveal Carmen, as well as a group of reporters behind her who are also trying to get in. Being the feisty little diva that she is, Carmen manages to hold them off while I let her in, half-blind from the countless camera flashes as I close the door behind her.

"What the hell was that about?" I ask, rubbing my eyes.

"Turn on the news and you'll find out."

"You do it, my eyes are still recuperating," I say, tossing the remote in what I can only hope is her direction. She turns the TV on and flicks over to a news channel, which seems to be covering the attempted armed robbery yesterday. She flicks to another, featuring the same story. Then another, and another. Most of them are showing a picture of me, and it's not a very flattering one.

"Where'd they get that gross picture of me, and why am *I* on the news?"

"Probably from your old Instagram account. You know you never deleted it, right?"

"Oh my god, you're joking! Help me delete it now!"

"Yeah, yeah, we'll get to that later, just shut up and listen! They're calling you a hero," she says, while I try to accept the fact that I'm an idiot who doesn't even know how to delete an Instagram account. Though, let's be honest, all social media companies make it much harder to *delete* an account than start one up.

"I'm not a hero," I say, to make it very clear that I don't want to take credit for something that me and you both know I didn't do out of selflessness.

"Of course you are! If it weren't for you being brave enough to stand up to those idiots, who knows what would have happened?"

"Just because I did something stupid that, on this occasion, happened to work out in our favour, doesn't mean I'm a hero," I explain.

"Brian, I get that you're trying to be modest, but just embrace it! I know you've been going through a hard time since the breakup, so let's just try and start fresh."

She's trying to lighten my mood, but she doesn't have a clue just how hard it's actually been. I wish I *was* brave enough to tell her the truth. But I'm not, so I guess I should just try and get on board with whatever nonsense this brings my way.

"Okay," I concede. "So, what am I supposed to do with my newfound *fame*?" I ask.

"I've actually already booked you in for an interview with *The Daily Brew*," she says with a smile of feigned innocence.

"You did *what*?"

"Well, they asked if I knew you, and I said that we're friends and colleagues. Then one thing led to another, and I said I'd represent you."

"So, you're my self-appointed manager now?" I chuckle.

"Yep, so go get showered and dressed. And for the love of God, brush those teeth, or eat a mint, at the very least," she sasses.

TOO LATE?

I gasp dramatically, holding my hand to my chest. "How dare you!"

"You know it's true," she says with side-eye. "Now, come on, hurry up! We need to leave in an hour."

"Alright, alright, I didn't realise you were going to be a *momager* about it. Besides, it's *The Daily Brew*. They're not exactly the most prestigious show on morning television. Don't they usually have stories like 'Dog Predicts Winner of the Super Bowl', and it's just some mutt deciding between a bowl of chicken or beef."

"Yes, but they also have a main, proper meaty story, pardon the pun, and today, that's you! So, get a move on! They're paying us *quite* handsomely, so quit complaining!"

"Girl! Why didn't you start with that?" I say, before rushing off to get ready. At first, I was reluctant to this whole idea, but now that there's *money* involved, dare I say it, I'm a little excited!

I jump in the shower and brush my teeth, even spoiling myself with a little flossing, before picking out the best outfit I can. I choose something that is slimming, just in case there are any prospective bachelors watching from home. However, it's almost lunch time on a weekday so, if they *are* watching, they're probably unemployed and living with their parents – and we don't want any of that. Then again, maybe I'm just subconsciously projecting because I'm still hurt that my parents want nothing to do with me, but that sounds like a problem for therapy.

"Come on! We're going to be late!"

"OMG, I'm coming!" I shout back like a teenager. As I step out of my room, Carmen gasps, and I panic. "What's wrong?"

"Brian, you look great!" she says, smiling.

Normally, I wouldn't appreciate the over-the-top reaction. But, to be fair, I hadn't looked or felt this good in a long time. Even in public I'd been dressing like a slob since the breakup. Perhaps Carmen is right. Perhaps this *is* the start of a new chapter for me.

"Let's go, I've got a taxi waiting outside. Let's hope that the pap got bored and left."

"The *pap*?"

"Yeah, it's lingo for paparazzi, duh."

"Yeah, I know that, thanks to Lady Gaga, but you shortening it makes you sound like a Kardashian. I think you're already *way* too into this," I laugh.

"I'm into it just enough," she replies proudly.

"Okay, whatever, let's go." I smile at her silliness. Even though she might not know what's going on in my crazy head, she still always makes me smile, just by being her usual quirky self. Carmen uses her unrivalled confidence and sass to part the paparazzi like Moses did the Red Sea, and though I'm sure a few them still got flashes of my double chin, we make it to the taxi relatively dignified. We clamber into the car, and make our way over Brooklyn Bridge to the rich streets of Manhattan, and thankfully not to work. Hopefully, if we milk this for all it's worth, we won't have to go back to that awful place.

Entering a large, extravagant building, we approach the fancy reception desk. Carmen takes the lead and does the talking, which is more than okay with me. I mean, if I had this kind of service all the time, I'd never have to deal

TOO LATE?

with my social anxiety. Carmen tells the receptionist who we are and what we're here for, while I hold back and contemplate everything that's happened in the last twenty-four hours. I've gone from wanting to kill myself – and don't get me wrong, there's still an overwhelming urge to do so – to being a guest on a talk show.

Carmen links arms with me before we waltz off to the elevator, popping a lanyard around my neck, as well as her own, as we head up to the thirtieth – yep, *thirtieth* – floor. The doors finally open to reveal the behind-the-scenes of a television studio, and there are way more people than I ever imagined. Most of them pass us without batting an eyelid, as I'm sure they have more important things to be doing. But suddenly, one of the passers-by backtracks his steps and turns to face us.

"You!" the even-sassier-than-me man says with his finger pointing at me, "You're the Bank Boy! Come with me!" he signals for us to follow, departing without warning. I look at Carmen, who is, quite obviously, trying not to laugh in my face. We both follow in his direction.

"It's not quite the nickname that *I* would've chosen," I say, quiet enough so that only Carmen can hear.

"I don't know what you mean, I think it's great," she replies, trying not to splutter with laughter.

"Let's get you in hair and makeup," the man says, waving his hand over his head in, what we assume, is a signal to keep following him.

"I thought I actually looked okay," I coyly mention to him.

He turns on his heel to look me up and down. "Yes, you do look . . . okay, but we want you to look *fabulous*! You too," he side-eyes Carmen, who is giggling at my expense. Then, he resumes his powerwalk to the makeup station.

"What?" Carmen chokes, and now it's *my* turn to laugh.

"Well, they want you on the sofa, too. Someone who was there, to corroborate Bank Boy's story. Right, here we are," he forcefully plops us down into two hair-and-makeup chairs, as two young women spin us around to face the mirrors.

"I did try to make my hair look good," I say to the lady who is standing behind my chair. Her reflection in the mirror simply smiles politely, yet unconvincingly, in reply. They fix us up in no time and, before I know it, I see an almost filtered version of myself in the mirror. In fairness, they have done a much better job than I ever could, and at least they haven't made me change clothes. I must've gotten something right. Either that, or more accurately they don't have anything to fit my huge ass.

"That was almost as much hair and makeup attention as when I had my quinceañera," Carmen mentions, as we're escorted to another area where we have a view of the main set.

"Oh my god, I wish I had known you back then. I bet your quinceañera was a blast!"

"Yeah, it really was, and I wish you'd been there too. I had friends, but none of them as weird as you," she smiles with a playful wink.

The show begins, and we watch from behind the scenes. All I know, up until now, is that our slot is after the first commercial break. We watch as they introduce the stories of the day, and I discover that we're sandwiched between 'The World's Biggest Strawberry' and, who would've guessed it, a dog that can predict the future. Me, I guessed it. Clearly, my story isn't as important as Carmen made out.

"Ooh, we're up next," Carmen says excitably.

"Yeah, luckily the giant strawberry story didn't over run," I utter sarcastically.

"Dude, they need some fluff stories to put around the main event."

"If you say so," I mutter, annoyed that I care.

We're ushered onto the sofa beside the host, who is a bubbly black lady named Jada Wilson, who has a beautiful head of braids with strands of white weaved into them. *The Daily Brew* have a plethora of hosts that they switch around every week to keep things fresh. Jada is the only one who ever hosts alone, though, I think that's because she's a boss-ass bitch. I know I slated the show earlier, but I often watch YouTube clips of Jada's interviews. The sassy man from before counts Jada back in as the commercials near their end and, before I know it, I'm live on national television.

"Welcome back to *The Daily Brew*! Here with me now, is the man who saved countless lives in the armed robbery yesterday just a few blocks away from this very building – Brian Christian, everyone!"

Yeah, don't worry, I know the irony of my last name and my parents and all that crap, that's why I didn't divulge that information to you earlier.

"We also have his best friend and co-worker, who happened to be on the scene when it all happened – Carmen Alvarez! So, tell me, how long have you guys known each other?" Jada directs the question to neither one of us in particular.

I freeze up and, thankfully, Carmen steps in. "About five years, give or take, right Brian?" She nudges me for confirmation.

"Oh, er . . . yeah, thereabouts. We met through work," I mutter robotically, as if I've forgotten how to talk like a functioning person.

"I see. And has Brian always been a selfless hero?" Jada asks Carmen. I think she sees that I'm clearly not going to be the conversationalist out of the two of us.

"To be completely honest, I didn't know he had it in him. But clearly, when push comes to shove, a hero he is," Carmen compliments. I think.

"That's incredible," Jada nods. "How about you, Brian? Did you know you were capable of such bravery?"

"I wouldn't really call it bravery. Stupidity, maybe. Or luck," I chuckle self-deprecatingly.

"Nonsense! What you did was extremely heroic! America wants to show you their appreciation! Accept it, Brian! You know, something tells me you're the kind of humble guy that doesn't take compliments very well," Jada says, as if she can see right into my soul and read me like an open book.

"Oh my god, you're *so* right," Carmen chimes in. "He *never* takes a compliment."

"Well, he's going to have to get used to it, isn't he?" Jada proposes to Carmen, and the imaginary audience. "Come on now, Brian. We need to get you accepting the compliments you deserve. After all, you're a fetching young man, you must get hit on all the time!"

"Not really," I awkwardly laugh it off.

TOO LATE?

"Yeah, because he hasn't been on a night out with me in *ages*," Carmen once again pipes up, dropping me in it.

"Well, that explains it! You're not getting any attention because you're keeping yourself hidden away! I'm quite sure that after this airs, the guys will be lining up to date the heroic Brian the Bank Boy," Jada beams.

I'm a little taken aback that she just assumed I'm gay. Thankfully, the camera pans over to her before my half-open mouth is caught on national television. She wraps up the segment with one last compliment that I'm too distracted to hear, before preparing to move onto the psychic dog.

"God, that's such a cringey nickname. I really hope it doesn't stick. Also, why did she just assume that I'm gay?" I whisper to Carmen as we get off the sofa.

"Dude, you *are* gay. *Extremely* gay. Also, 'sexuality' was on one of the forms that I had to fill out for you to get this gig."

"Okay, you make two fair points."

"Come on, let's get out of here and find this *queue* of boys that are waiting to jump your bones," Carmen sniggers.

"Hey, Jada thinks I'm a catch." I nudge her in the arm.

"So do I! *You're* the one who doesn't believe it! But hopefully, after you've had a couple of dicks in you, you'll start to feel better."

"Did you just say dicks?" I chuckle.

"No. I said *drinks*," she says. suspiciously looking to the side.

"I don't know, I mean, it *does* sound tempting . . . but —"

"But nothing! You, me, out, tonight!"

"Okay, okay. Fine," I concede.

In the literal hours after my interview with Jada, my socials start to skyrocket, and I've now gone from a couple hundred followers, to over ten thousand! Upon very scrupulous inspection, the majority of them seem to be hunky guys. Maybe Jada was right. Maybe I *am* a catch. And . . . *maybe* . . . my failed suicide attempt was the best thing to ever happen to me.

Maybe.

CHAPTER 4

ME, MYSELF, AND MY THERAPIST

It's been about a week since my television interview, and I've had many sexual encounters of late. At first, it was fun. *Very* fun. But it soon became apparent that I was only getting that kind of attention because everyone thinks that I'm some courageous hero, which you and I both know is far from the truth. The reality of the matter is that I am a coward.

I know, I can hear you shouting out right now, "no, you're not!"

But I am.

I ran as far away from my parents as possible instead of sticking up for myself and fighting back. I let my stupid ex literally just walk away with my dog. And, well, you know what *actually* happened at the bank. I am a coward, and I accepted that fact a long time ago. Bravery is overrated anyway. It either gets you into trouble or killed which, ironically, is the one thing that I wasn't blessed with from my own act of 'bravery'.

The endless stream of partners, providing good but ultimately pointless sex, has become just that – pointless. I had my slut era in high school, remember, so I don't need or even just desire my current situation. I think I just got carried away with all the attention. I mean, it *had* been a long time since I'd been touched by another guy, so at least my little stint has got me back on the horse, so to speak. Or rather, a guy with a dick the size of a horse. *Seriously*, you should've seen some of these guys!

Now though, I'm kind of feeling a bit gross about it all. Every encounter was based on a lie, and I don't think that'll pan out very well for my mental health later down the line. So, I decided to book in with my therapist. I'm supposed to see her every week but, for one, she can't make me, and two, you remember how much it costs, right? I'm not forking out one hundred and fifty dollars every week! So instead, I just book in when I see fit, and right now, unfortunately, I definitely see fit to do so. My appointment is booked for today, and I'm actually going to be late so, I better go.

***

I'm currently having to walk to my therapy appointment because my bike is in the workshop. They've apparently fixed it, but every time I call to arrange a pickup time,

TOO LATE?

they try to sell me all of these upgrades – bells and whistles, literally. They're essentially holding it hostage, and the ransom price seems to be me purchasing one of their white shopping baskets to mount on the front.

Would that be really useful for me? Yes, of course it would, and I think they look really cute. But, the principal of the matter is that I won't allow them to think they've won one over me, which they *will* if I cave and buy one.

Thus, I'm leaving my bike with them for a few more days as I simply can't be fucked with the drama of it all. Luckily, I live in New York, so nothing is ever too far away. After a half hour walk – which, knowing my luck probably didn't even burn a single calorie – I arrive at my therapist's office.

The building itself isn't anything spectacular so I really don't know what my one hundred and fifty dollars is being spent on as it's certainly not her wardrobe, either. Sorry, that was shady. That's my *Drag Race* side coming out.

Drag Race has this way of turning its fans into queer little Simon Cowells, thinking we can just go around judging everyone. And it doesn't matter that I'm currently dressed like a slob because I'm the one who needs mental help. She, however, is a professional, and should have better attire. Having said that, I really hope the stain on my joggers is toothpaste.

I walk into the building, visit reception as usual, and am directed to the waiting area. This is when I'm reminded of the fact that my therapist shares the building with a dentist. A dentist who mainly offers small aesthetic surgeries like lip filler and Botox so, are they even really a dentist? This means that the waiting room is usually filled with two types of people –cosmetic virgins, whose lips are wafer-thin and cheeks saggy and, cosmetic veterans/addicts, whose lips are already twice the size of a baboon's ass and yet they're back for more.

Having just slated them all, they're actually a great bunch of people to talk to. Especially the 'virgins', as they don't quite have the confidence to be passive-aggressive yet. And when I say talk to, by the way, I mean I sit there and eavesdrop on their conversations for entertainment. You didn't think I'd willingly subject myself to the crippling anxiety of making small talk in a patient's waiting room, did you?

Thankfully, due to the hour-long sessions, and my therapist being the only therapist in the building, I never have to mingle with any other *like-minded* people. My own problematic mental health is enough to deal with, without taking on someone else's problems while we both wait to be 'fixed' by the doc.

I did notice, last time I was here, that the dentist also does armpit Botox. I might inquire about it one of these days. And no, I'm not oddly vain about my armpits, it's just that it's supposed to stop excessive sweating. And boy oh boy, do I have excessive sweating! I walk down a set of stairs – I sweat. I kick a ball once – I sweat. I sit on the couch and watch television – I sweat, and, if I'm in any setting that makes me even *remotely* socially anxious, which I'm in almost every second of every day, you guessed it – I sweat.

I wouldn't mind if it was only a little bit, but it's literally buckets of salty bodily fluids pouring out of every inch of my skin. The only thing that's stopping me from getting Botox is that apparently it hurts like a bitch. Oh, and it's hella expensive! I'll look more into it when I free up some cash after I've 'graduated' therapy, if that ever happens. Maybe *then* I'll be able to afford the luxury of paying someone to stab my armpits on a regular basis.

Twenty minutes after my appointment was supposed to start, my therapist finally walks out with her last patient, whose eyes look so sore from crying that it seems like they've been staring at the sun for the past hour.

My therapist calls my name, even though I'm sat right next to her. Brenda is a lady of average height, shoulder length ginger curls and thick framed glasses. She gives weird-auntie-who's-not-technically-related-to-you vibes which, I guess, is kind of what a therapist is. Some nosey, estranged family friend.

"Hi," she says with a smile as if she hasn't kept me waiting, and I don't reply as I follow her into the office. "Take a seat," she gestures to the chair that I've sat in many times before. I don't know why she's treating me like a newb, I'm basically a pro at therapy. "How have you been?" she asks.

Oh yeah, great, fine, that's why I decided to book an appointment, just to have a gas, Brenda.

"I'm okay," I say with sass, trying really hard not to roll my eyes at her.

"And what does *okay* mean, in this instance?"

"It means, I'm okay."

It really means that I hate my life, Brenda, jeez. Read between the lines, it's literally your job. I'm too much of a mess to just tell you everything without you having to work for it.

"Brian, have you been taking your..." her words are slow and drawn out, as if she's scared to ask.

"Yes, I've been taking my meds."

I definitely have not.

"That's great! Make sure you stay on track with them, I think that they'll really help." I just nod in reply. "So, Brian, I heard about what happened to you at the bank. I'm guessing that's why you've booked an appointment? I want to know, how are you dealing with it all?" she enquires with a concerned look as she props up her notebook, preparing to scribble lines about how crazy I am.

"I wasn't scared, if that's what you mean," I reply truthfully.

"Well, it's a lot more complex than that, Brian. You were put into a fight-or-flight scenario in real life with real life, serious consequences. Whenever we've spoken about this matter in the past, you always claimed to be more of a 'flight' type of person, which most people are, and there is nothing wrong with that."

"What's your point, Doc?" I feel like she's low-key insulting me here.

"I just find it intriguing as to why, on this occasion, you took the 'fight' stance?" she says with squinted eyes, pulling her glasses down slightly as if trying to read my mind.

"I guess it's one thing to theorise about it, and another to actually experience it firsthand." I try my best to brush the question off, but she's persistent.

"I understand that but, still, it just seems... out of character."

TOO LATE?

"What's that supposed to mean?" Wow, she really isn't letting this whole bank thing go, is she?

"Brian, we both know how much you've struggled with your mental health and, usually, you're very self-involved with your mental illness. It's a complete departure to then do something so brave and selfless," she says, further adding insult to injury.

Oh my! This sassy bitch is really calling me out! Wait, why am I only saying this to you? I'm going to tell *her* she's being rude.

"Well, that's rude!" I say.

See. Told her.

"Brian, I'm not trying to upset you. I'm merely trying to address the facts that I believe, deep down, you know are true, too," she speaks calmly.

She's right, isn't she? She can see right through the bullshit 'hero' façade that the media has given me, and it *is* what I came here to talk about. I need to tell her. I need someone else to know what really happened.

"Okay, fine. You're right. I'm not brave, I'm not a hero, and I'm not selfless like everyone now thinks I am. I'm a coward." I stop to wipe my cheeks as the inevitable tears start to flow.

"What are you trying to tell me, Brian?" she asks softly.

"I wanted to die," I admit. "I stood there, and told the person holding a gun to my face to shoot me. When it was quiet enough for *just* them to hear, I made it clear that I wanted to die, but now everyone thinks I was doing it out of bravery. I wasn't! I just wanted an easy way out, because I know I'd never be able to do it to myself. And now, I have this overwhelming sense of imposter syndrome, because every guy that I meet thinks I'm something I'm not."

I finish my rant as Brenda slides a box of tissues across the coffee table between us. I thank her, spluttering through my tears. She looks through her notes while the air fills with silence. Well, other than the sound of me blowing my nose like a whale hole.

"Brian, do you still have suicidal thoughts?" she asks, breaking the awkward silence with an even more awkward question.

"Yeah. But also no. I don't know how to explain it. Yes, they're still there but I know I'll never act upon it, that's why I asked them to, at the bank," I answer honestly.

"And why do you feel like you won't act upon such feelings by yourself?"

"Because I'm too much of a chicken. Like you said, I'm 'flight'," I admit, deflated.

"Brian, you're not a chicken. I believe that deep down you care for others, and you *are* brave. I think that's the reason you haven't succeeded in killing yourself. It's because you know that there are people who would be distraught if you were to pass, and you can't bring yourself to leave them."

"I don't think so," I answer solemnly.

"Look, Brian, I'll be honest. I have never, in all my years, had such a truly unique case as yours. Unfortunately, though I've helped many people get their lives back on track, I have also lost people to their mental health struggles. Out of all the people I've seen, no one has ever been presented with a second chance at life like you have here. So, everyone thinks you're a hero, and

TOO LATE?

maybe that isn't true. But it doesn't matter what your intentions were in that moment. What matters is where you go from *here*. You can mope around, and feel sorry for yourself, and be engulfed by imposter syndrome. Or you can use this opportunity to become the person that everyone thinks you are. There's no rule book to life, Brian. Everyone's just faking it till they make it, myself included. I may look like someone who has it all together but even *I* have a therapist. I think everyone should have one, to be honest."

Not at one hundred and fifty dollars an hour they shouldn't.

I guess she's right in what she's saying. I *do* have a chance to reinvent myself. I can go back to being the confident kid I was in school, instead of this shell of a person that I've become. I'm locally famous now. None of these people know who I used to be, and they don't *need* to know. I can be anyone that I want to be. I can be the real *me*.

"Are you listening?" she asks, snapping me out of my internal epiphany.

"Yeah, sorry," I answer, my eyes sparking back to life.

"Okay, good. Now, having said all that, please remember to keep taking your medication. It will help your anxiety, especially."

"Thanks, Doc," I let out a little smile.

"You're welcome. Now, I want you to come in at least every two weeks for the time being, so we can monitor your unkind thoughts. And, if you *do* ever feel the urge to harm yourself – or worse – you can call me, okay?" she reassures with genuine sincerity.

"Yeah, okay. Bye," I smile before leaving. She must've brushed up on her therapy skills lately, because this might be the first time that I've found one of these sessions actually useful. Maybe she's getting tips from her own therapist.

I've decided that I'm going to take her advice – starting with no more meaningless sex. I'm going to start dating, and get braver about asking guys out. I waste so much time waiting around, pining over cute guys and hoping they'll ask me out, when I'm fully capable of making the first move. And hopefully, if I do as the doc says and actually take my pills, then maybe that will make everything easier, too. And, if none of that works, I can always go back to my depressive state of self-hatred. Really, it's a win-win.

I begin walking home and, you know, it's true what they say. Fresh, traffic-polluted air in New York really does the soul some good. I'm about two blocks away from my apartment when I hear a rustle coming from some trash down a side street, and turn to see what looks like the butt of a dog rummaging through some trash bags.

It hears me, and shimmies itself out of the pile of garbage to face me. The dog has an empty packet of chips hanging from the corner of its mouth and its bottom lip is cutely tucked under its teeth. It is adorable, and clearly not much older than a pup. I edge closer, trying not to spook it.

"Hey there," I say, in the cute voice that all dog parents use when talking to their furry friends, and it looks up to me with literal puppy-dog eyes. I hold my hand out limply to show that I don't mean any harm, and the dog drops the chip packet and waddles over to me. I

TOO LATE?

can't quite tell what breed it is as I stroke it and it snuggles up to my feet. I'm assuming it's a mongrel, but it's so fluffy and adorable that I don't care what its concoction of breeds are – I want to keep it. There's no collar, but it could still have a chip.

"Come on, buddy, let's take you home and get you some proper food." Upon picking it up, I can see that it's a girl. Maybe she will make for a better companion than the treacherous male mongrel that abandoned me.

"No, you won't abandon me, will you?" I ask rhetorically to the little cutie as I hold her up to my face. Whisking my new pup back to my apartment, I feed her some of Copper's old food and call the vets to arrange an appointment, wanting to give her a once-over, and to see if she is chipped or not. I'm really hoping the answer is 'not'. For tonight, at least, I can pretend she's mine as we cuddle up on the couch and watch a romcom together.

***

It's the next day, and we're now in the vet's reception area. It's the same place we used to bring Copper, but I made sure to book in with one of the other vets so it won't be awkward. The old vet was a snooty bitch, anyway, always trying to upsell me one thing or another, and you might be thinking that she's a vet and knew what Copper needed, but the receptionist always stopped me from being scammed. Honestly, I think that vet missed her true calling in life, she should've been a car salesperson or something.

I'm booked in with a different vet who, according to Anne the receptionist, is a relatively new addition to the practice. Anne is a cute old lady whose silver hair is as luxurious as some of the pedigree dog's coats in the waiting room. Though, she's more of a cat person, she tells me, having two Siamese cats of her own.

She was more than happy to see me again, and when I told her what happened with my ex, she was definitely on my side. She even said she'd make him wait extra-long next time that he asks for an appointment – unless, of course, it's urgent, and stupid Copper is going to die or something. We're not *evil*.

As I sit here, anxiously awaiting my appointment, I wonder if this is how people on *Jerry Springer* feel when they're waiting for their DNA test results. My fingers are crossed that this puppy is homeless, and then I can indeed be the father, or at least adoptive father. I wait around endlessly for this mystery vet to call my name and then . . .

Oh my fucking god!

The vet appears in front of me, calling my name, but I'm too stunned to speak. Why didn't Anne *prepare* me by telling me that the new vet is an absolute *smoke show*?

Hello Mr Vet!

He's gorgeous, and just my type – tall, dark and handsome. His hair is relatively short and floppy, and his tanned jaw has the perfect length of stubble. Plus, those tight-fitting vet scrubs are *really* doing something to me right now!

"Brian, Brian Christian?" he calls out, snapping me out of my trance.

"Oh, er . . . that's me," I fumble my words.

He looks down at me with a smile. "Hi. Come on through."

TOO LATE?

I pick up my pup and follow him, trying not to faint from the scent of his intoxicatingly sexy cologne as we enter the room, and he pulls up my appointment details on his monitor. Quickly giving them a scan, he turns back around and pats on the tall stainless-steel table with a smile, indicating for me to place her down.

"So, just a once-over and check for a chip, correct?" he asks, admiring how cute the dog is.

"Yeah."

"Awesome. So, where'd you find this little beauty?" he begins inspecting her.

"In the trash," I say, nonchalantly.

"Oh no! Who would do that to such a little cutie," he says in the same voice I use when I talk to her, and when he picks her up with his bulging biceps, I think I finally understand the obsession with a DILF. Is this what girls feel when they see a guy with a baby? After a few more minutes of me watching and drooling over him, he comes to a conclusion.

"Luckily, she's looking pretty healthy and happy, although, I'd like to give her a booster shot as I'm not sure if she ever got one. Oh, and I would highly recommend that you give her a bath," he jokes, causing me to laugh way too intensely.

"Is she homeless?" I ask, to which he chuckles, though I'm being deadly serious.

"She doesn't have a chip, if that's what you mean?"

"Yeah, you say *tomayto* I say tomato."

That makes him chuckle again. Is this him flirting? Because I've been told that I'm not actually very funny, and when people laugh at not-funny things, it's because they like you, right? Okay, I'm getting off topic. Let's focus on the dog.

"So . . . can I keep her?"

"Sure, but it's a big responsibility to take in a dog. If you like, I can keep her in overnight if you want to think about it?" he says, petting her.

"Oh, thanks, but there's no need. I've had a dog before and, I know it sounds silly, and *super* gay but, I'm convinced now that me and her were supposed to meet."

"Okay, well, in that case, would you like me to chip her now for you?"

"Yeah, sure," I smile appreciatively.

"What name will it be?" he asks as he turns to the computer, ready to fill in the details.

"Er . . . Brian."

"Oh no, sorry! I meant *her* name," he smiles, glancing at the dog.

"Sorry, my bad," I awkwardly laugh. "Erm . . . Lucky." I answer confidently.

"I like it," he smiles, before turning back to the computer.

"Thanks."

God he's so hot! Should I ask him out?

This is what I was talking about before. I just stew and wait around, but I *should* ask him, right? Although, are you allowed to date your vet? Surely, it's fine. He's treating my dog, not me. Although, I do wish he'd look after me, too, if you catch my drift. But what if he says no? That would be too embarrassing – and I'd have to change vets *again*. No, it's definitely best to keep things platonic. No romance whatsoever. Strictly nothing. Nada.

TOO LATE?

"Hey, do you maybe want to go–" he begins, but I cut him off.

"Out? Yes!"

Shit! What just happened? I literally just said I wasn't going to do that! Damn my mouth! Oh my god! Either time has frozen, or *he* has, because nothing is happening. We're both just staring at each other in shock.

Please say something!

"Oh," he utters. *'Oh', isn't good.* "I was going to say, do you want to settle the bill out front with Anne, and I'll bring Lucky out in a minute?" he looks embarrassed enough for the both of us.

I. Am. *Mortified*. How do I come back from that? Okay, think about what Brenda said – fake it till you make it! I'll just laugh it off, pretend it was a joke. Also, I know I wanted him to say something but in my fantasy world he was going to say 'yes' not 'oh.'

"Ha! I was just joking with you," I awkwardly laugh, and he smiles to be polite, but I can see straight through it. "Anyway, I'll go wait out there," I say, as I'm already halfway out the door.

"I'm so stupid," I mutter to myself as I walk down the hallway back to the reception. How did I think that someone like *that* would've been into *me*? I should've learned my lesson by now. I go see Anne and silently pay my bill before a nurse brings Lucky to me. Clearly, he's too embarrassed by the encounter to even look at me and, to be fair, I don't blame him.

Lucky and I head home and cuddle up once more on the couch. "At least she's officially mine now," I say out loud, to remind myself, as I pull out my phone and start a web search for a new veterinary practice.

CHAPTER 5

A FRESH START

A few days have passed since the awkward situation at the vets and, somehow, I've not died of the consequent embarrassment. Lucky is settling in great, and we're getting on like a house on fire. Thankfully, there's nothing wrong with her at the moment, medically speaking, meaning that I can chill out on the search for a new vet.

Carmen messaged last night, asking if I wanted to go on a night out like the good old days. At first, I was like 'no'. But, after reevaluating my life – and seeing as how trying to meet people *naturally* isn't going well – I suppose a gay bar might be my only chance. So, I said yes.

I mean, is it really *that* out of the realm of possibility that a relatively hot guy could like me? I have great

TOO LATE?

boyfriend skills! I can cook, I'm great at sex, I think, and . . . okay so that might be all the skills that I have but – food and sex! What more do they want? Anyway, tonight is the night where I meet my new future husband. I just hope that *he* doesn't also turn out to be a dirty, lying cheat who steals my new dog.

Speaking of dogs, I've got some time to kill before Carmen gets here, and Lucky needs a walk. It'll also give me a chance to do some online job hunting. The payout from the bank, combined with the fee for the television interview, has allowed me a month off from work without stressing about finances. However, that window is rapidly closing, and I can't think of anything worse than going back to ABA Bank. Even though my best friend works there, neither of us enjoy it, and I think one of us needs to leave to push the other out the door, too. So, I'm hoping I can bag myself a new job before time's up.

I'm walking along with Lucky's lead in one hand and my phone in the other as I scroll through a job-search website. I *hate* job-search websites. You put your criteria into the page, and they basically just ignore it all. I entered 'New York' as my ideal location and listed my qualifications, and they *still* have the audacity to tease me with jobs like 'doctor'.

It's almost as if they *know* that I'm a greedy dumbass who looks at the salaries first and the job title second. So, I get all excited that a well-paid job has popped up within my criteria, to then find out that it's for a pissing neurosurgeon in London. In tiny italic writing under the job advert, it says:

'You may be lacking some of the qualifications needed for this role.'

Yeah, well, no shit.

They're the ones trying to convince me to be a cybersecurity analyst, professor, or CEO, when they know I'm far too unqualified for any of those jobs. Yet, I'm still *clearly* smarter than them, as I wouldn't send people jobs that are out of their league in the first place. Well, I better put my phone away as I can now see some trampy dog trying to hump my precious Lucky.

"Hey! Beat it!" I shout clapping my hands together. The little scruff runs off, and it's only now that I'm realising it looks familiar. No . . . it can't be. Can it? Oh my god, it is! That used to be *my* trampy dog! It's Copper! Which means that the owner he's running to is . . . oh my god! Ben's there, and he's with his twinky whore of a boyfriend!

"Lucky, come!" I call out, as I back into the shrubbery and pray to whoever's in charge of this cruel world to hide me. Lucky shimmies through the bushes and snuggles up by my feet just in time to avoid attention, and I can just about see Ben and his twink through the branches and leaves. Ugh, they're so gross! And their PDA is far too much! They're practically *humping* each other out in public! They're worse than the dogs! I watch as they walk .

Shit. I'm going to snee–
"ACHOO!"
They definitely hear me and start walking back.

"Hello? Who's there? Wait, Brian? Is that *you*?" Ben calls out to the bush I'm hiding in.

"Oh, hey! Sorry," I say, walking out. "I didn't see you there! Lucky took a crap in the bushes, so I was just being a responsible pet owner."

TOO LATE?

I think Lucky just gave me side-eye, the sassy bitch. She needs to learn that she has to take the fall sometimes, for her daddy's sake.

"Er . . . okay. How've you been?" Ben asks, his arm still firmly wrapped around the twink's waist. Which, I might add, is literally the size of a twig. See, I knew he didn't like me because I put on weight!

"I'm fine. I've actually got a new boyfriend, too," I blurt out, even though no one remotely asked about my relationship status.

"Awesome! I'm glad you're moving on," he answers, with a smile that looks sincere, but I know him well enough to know it's fake, and I *really* cannot be bothered with this fake sincerity right now. Ben doesn't care about me, he never did.

"Yeah, well, I guess I just needed someone who *gets* me," I say passive-aggressively.

Ben passes his boyfriend Copper's lead and says he'll catch up in a second. His boyfriend gives Ben a pouty look. Ben grossly sticks his tongue down his throat before reassuring him.

"Don't worry," he says in a sickly-sweet voice, which kinda makes me want to vomit. His boyfriend finally leaves and Ben then walks up to me with what appears to be a genuine look of care in his eyes. "How are you really doing, Brian?"

"Like you care," I try to brush him off.

"Look, I know we weren't the perfect match, and I know I was a dick. I've realised that now. But I *did* care about you." Is he being nice, or did I hit my head? "How are you . . . mentally?"

"Er . . . better than I was." Or at least I think I am.

"I know I'm probably the last person you'd want to talk to, but my number hasn't changed if you ever need an ear to listen," he offers with a comforting smile.

"Thanks, Ben," I smile, though I'm not sure I'd ever actually want to talk to him about anything.

He walks off to catch up with his boyfriend, and I look down at Lucky with a weirded-out expression on my face. I'm pretty sure she gives me the same look back.

Well, that was not what I was expecting, but it felt good to have a little more closure over Ben. He's right, we both are. We just weren't meant to be, and that's okay. Especially because tonight, I will be moving on, and then hopefully *next time* I bump into him, I'll have a *real* boyfriend to tell him about.

The rest of our walk is thankfully uneventful, other than Lucky taking a giant, steaming turd. I actually quite enjoy walking around with a bag full of poo, it makes me feel safer. I mean, think about it. What if, on my way back home, someone tries to mug me? They'd be met with a face full of dog shit! I only have one block left to go, though, so I dump the bag in a stranger's trashcan.

I get home and fill up Lucky's food and water bowls before starting to get ready. I pull out some skinny jeans, and a nice shirt from my wardrobe, laying them on my bed – even though skinny jeans aren't cool anymore and I don't know when *that* happened. I take my second shower of the day, because my *relaxing* walk in the park ended up giving me anxiety sweats and now I stink. I get dressed just in time to let Carmen in when she buzzes.

Once she's in my apartment, I introduce her to Lucky, and explain the whole predicament at the vets *and* the earlier exchange with Ben.

TOO LATE?

"So, what I'm hearing is, you need your wing woman back?" she says with a cheeky grin.

"Yes, but this time I want a *nice* guy to date! Not just a one-night stand. I want to chat to cute guys and . . . network."

"Network? We're finding you a new man, not a job."

"Well, I *am* in need of both, so if we can kill two birds with one stone, that'd be great."

"Don't worry, I have the perfect idea!"

"Which is?" I prompt, but she gives nothing away.

"A surprise, thank you very much."

"Hmm, okay," I say, feigning a scowl.

We get the pre-drinks started with a couple of pink-gin-and-lemonades while we scroll through each other's Tinder profiles.

"Need a top up?" Carmen asks, waving her empty glass as she holds out her hand for mine.

"Ooh, yes!" She takes my glass and heads to the fridge to fix us up some more drinks. "Hey, I'm just going to go ahead and do some swiping for you," I shout out, to wind her up.

"You better not! I need to verify all the riffraff that you're matching me with!"

"Oh my god, I got you an instant match! Wow, he's actually kinda hot. I'll admit, I didn't notice at first because I was just swiping everybody right," I call out, laughing.

"You're such an idiot, and now *this* is your punishment." Her smile is devilish as she turns around with our gins on a tray – accompanied by an eclectic collection of shots. There are far too many colours and consistencies on that tray for my liking. Does she realise we're not eighteen anymore? Not that we were drinking at eighteen, of course, because that would be illegal. Insert wink here.

"No! Not shots! Please, I beg of you! I'll be wasted before we even get to the club!" I plea. "And where'd you even find all of these?" I ask, knowing that I haven't seen some of these liquids in years.

"You'll need some liquid courage for what I have planned. And as for the drinks, some I brought, and others I found at the back of your liquor cabinet. But, to be honest, the bottles were pretty dusty, and I'm not sure that *this* one is supposed to look that . . . creamy," she laughs, pointing at the cloudy beige shot.

I gag just looking at it. "Jesus, we're going to die."

"Oh, come on! We're no lightweights. Now, the game is–"

"There's a game?" I interrupt.

"*Yes*, if you'd let me finish. The game is that we keep swiping each other's profiles, but if there's one we really don't like, then you have to do a shot, or forfeit, and let them be swiped right."

"Okay, challenge accepted!" I say, handing her my phone.

"Famous last words," she smiles.

I'm the first to cave and take a shot as Carmen tries to swipe a 'short king' for me. I have nothing against short guys, but when you're a six-foot bottom, it's not really the vibe. And you can go on about personality as much as you want, of course it matters, but I'm a very sexual person so, if I'm not attracted to them then there's no point wasting either person's time.

TOO LATE?

I accept my punishment and go to grab a shot of something that at least looks a bit fruity, but, last-minute, Carmen changes the rules.

"No, you have to take *this* one. The other person gets to pick the shot," she says, smiling proudly as she hands me a shot of what looks like sambuca. I literally can't think of anything worse. Reluctantly, I neck the syrupy tar-like substance and instantly wretch, feeling it burning my insides as it goes down. I take a sip of my gin to rid the rancid taste from my mouth, while scowling at Carmen, who just laughs.

However, my face swiftly lights up once more as me and Carmen simultaneously lock eyes on her next possible match. There's nothing wrong with him, he's actually rather handsome, but he also looks like a douchebag. Looking through his photos, we see that he has a picture of himself with his arms folded in front of yacht that seems to be called *Tig Old Bitties*, another of him posing next to a dead lion that he's just shot, and his profile just says, 'looking for a girl that makes good sandwiches.'

It really couldn't get any worse for Carmen, and I'm even considering letting her have a free pass on this one. *But*, she created the game, so it only seems fair that she follows the same rules. Being a good sport, she accepts her punishment.

"Here, take this one," I say holding out the creamy, curdled, and clearly past-it's-due-date shot.

"Aw, crap! I was hoping to make this *your* next one," she sighs. Stupidly, she takes a whiff of it beforehand, and almost chunders there and then.

"Bottoms up!" I encourage.

***

A few more shots and dodgy profiles later, and it's eleven p.m. – finally time for the club. Carmen calls us a cab and, before long, we're in a gay club on a Tuesday night where, funnily enough, there's a drag queen hosting a speed dating night for gay guys.

"Hey, so I signed you up, you're welcome," Carmen says, returning from the bar with two drinks in hand, not that either of us really need any more alcohol coursing through our veins.

"What? No! This is so lame! I don't want to sit through loads of random guys. I'll probably only fancy one. Or if I do fancy more, they won't like me back."

"Come on, just give it a go!"

"No, I'm sorry, it's too embarrassing! Even *I'm* not that much of a loser!" I moan, stepping back to avoid the name badge that Carmen is insisting she pin on me when I bump into someone behind me.

"So, you think speed dating is for losers?" a sexy, somewhat familiar, voice asks.

I turn to see *him*.

The vet!

My eyes widen in shock and, from his point of view, I must look like a deer in headlights right now.

"I guess I'm a loser, then," he says, pointing at the name badge pinned to his hunky, buff chest. I'm still speechless, as I'm scared that, if I open my mouth, I'll only make things worse with whatever verbal diarrhoea ensues. In my stunned silence, Carmen sneakily attaches my own badge, poking me in the tit while she does it.

"Ow!" I blurt.

TOO LATE?

"Guess I'll be seeing you out there," he says, looking closely at my badge before heading to the set-up area for the speed dating. It's only now that I manage to get a glance at *his* name badge. I hadn't even thought about his name until now. I just called him 'Mr Vet' in my mind. But there it is, pinned to him – LOGAN. As in Wolverine from *X-Men*. I can't think of anything hotter.

"Dude, he was so hot! Do you know him?" Carmen asks.

"He's *the* vet!"

"Oh my god, no!" she replies, now mirroring the mortified, embarrassed look I'm sure is on my own face. "Dude, that must've been so awkward."

"Yeah, thanks, I'm aware," I mutter, rolling my eyes.

Carmen places her hands on my shoulders and attempts to psyche me up. "Look, just go out there and have fun! Make him jealous!"

"I really don't think he's going to be jealous over *me*," I say, with a depressive sigh.

"Well, I've already paid your entry fee, so get your ass over there!" She swivels me around by my shoulders before patting my butt.

"Alright, alright, fine." I give in, and head over to the group of mostly-attractive men awaiting instructions. The drag queen running the event is called Cherry Cola, who looks about seven-feet tall, with a huge ginger wig and a glitter beard. She's rocking every bit of it. Sometimes, I wish I could be a drag queen. I've already got the curves for it, annoyingly.

Cherry Cola points at seemingly random men, and assigns them to tables that have been placed in a circle where the main dance floor would usually be. Logan is one of those men. The rest of us are told that *we* will be the ones moving, switching to the next table along every ninety seconds.

"Everyone find a table to start at and when I play this noise," Cherry Cola instructs, playing a noise from their DJ setup that sounds like a clown's horn, "change and move clockwise to your next guy. There's no lingering at a table, and no leaving early, everyone must get a fair chance. Now, off you go!"

I notice two things as I get a good look at the group of men. One is that the tabled men don't seem so random anymore. Cherry clearly tried to put the tables as the tops and the movers as the bottoms. It's so obvious and, it's a little stereotypical that, of course, all the twinks are bottoms. Then again, I'm an oversized twink and a bottom, so clearly Cherry Cola just has a sixth sense about these things.

The second thing I notice is that I'm lumbered with a start position that's five tables away from Logan. Though, to be honest, I'm not sure if that's a good thing or not. What's going to happen when I get to his table? Is he just going to reject me again? Maybe he'll give me a second chance? Either way, the suspense is going to kill me, so let's hope that these other dates go really quick, even by speed dating standards.

I sit down with the first guy, who is actually pretty hot. I ask him what he does for a living and those are the last words I get in before he proceeds to talk about himself for the next eighty-five seconds. Thankfully, the noise is played, and I can move on to the next guy in the lineup. He's not my type at all, so I decide to just try and take a friendly approach rather than a flirty one and wait out the next ninety seconds. After the initial introduction, he also acts in a more friendzone way.

"You don't fancy me, do you?" I ask.

"You're handsome, but not my type, sorry," the blonde surfer-dude answers.

"No, don't worry, I don't like you either," I say it with too much enthusiasm, making it sound mean. "Sorry, I just meant you're not my type either."

"That's alright," he chuckles. "Can I be honest?" he asks, leaning in a little closer.

"Yeah, sure," I encourage.

"I know I give off top vibes, and I'm pretty sure that's why I got a table, but I'm actually a bottom," he whispers.

"See, I knew we'd been positioned like that! Why don't you see if any of the bottoms are actually tops and swap places?" I propose.

"That's a great idea, or even a verse at the very least. So, who *is* your type?" he asks, flirting his eyes at the circle of guys around us.

"That one over there," I say trying to point to Logan without making it obvious.

"Oof, yes girl, he is a snack! Go get him before I do!" he teases.

The ninety seconds are up, and I move on. The next two guys are clearly only in it for a quick shag, which is fine for them, but I'm obviously not doing any 'spiritual connecting' here. The exaggerated honking sound plays and I move on to the penultimate table. Or at least it *will be* penultimate, if I'm classing Logan as my final destination and ignoring the five other guys after that. Which I am.

As I take my seat, I get a whiff of the final guy's breath and it absolutely reeks. I turn my head away from his direction and catch a glimpse of Carmen smiling at me with two enthusiastic thumbs-up. I scowl back. It's her fault I'm partaking in this sick form of torture.

Now, don't get me wrong, my morning breath is that toxic it could kill, but if you're planning on trying to pull on a night out, at least have the common decency to pop a mint in your mouth beforehand. As he barks his credentials at me, spit, and a cloud of hot toxic breath, hits me in the face. By this point, though, I'm no longer phased by it because I can't take my eyes off of Logan.

All I can think about is whether he's enjoying his date with that little hoe-bag across from him. Sorry, that was mean. I'm sure he's not a hoe-bag, and I really shouldn't be tearing down other gay guys, there's enough homophobes out there already without me helping. Having said that, the slut better get his filthy paws off my vet's arm. Luckily, the sound once again plays before he can get any closer, and I can leave my table, free to breathe once more.

I stand up and turn to the man whose breath smells like he's been eating dog shit for breakfast, lunch, and dinner his whole life, and silently hand him a mint before moving on. It may seem rude, but so is the hate crime emanating from his mouth. Besides, I just saved the next twink a whole lot of hurt and trauma. So, really, it's a selfless act.

I quickly fix my hair, even though I have no way of seeing it right now, and finally sit at Logan's table. As I do, I soon realise that I had never decided on whether this

TOO LATE?

was going to be a good or bad outcome and thus the anxiety takes control instantly, fusing my mouth shut.

"Hey," he smiles.

"H-hey," I just about manage to utter. It's as if the words are in a prison and my pursed lips are the cell bars.

"Listen, about the other day–"

"No, don't even worry about it! I'm sorry that I was so forward. You clearly don't like me like that, and that's fine. I'll find a new vet and you'll never have to see me again," I blurt out frantically, my eyes darting about as my hands end up on either side of my face.

"Woah, that was a lot. You *really* need to stop cutting me off and answering questions I haven't asked yet," Logan smiles.

"Sorry," I mutter, looking down and dropping my hands under the table so they can anxiously fidget.

"I never said I didn't like you–"

"But–" I stop myself this time as I realise I'm about to cut him off again after he's just asked me not to. He gives me a stern, almost sexy, look, but it slowly softens as I allow him to finish his sentence.

"I *do* like you. I was just too shy to ask you out. Well, I *was* going to ask you out, but when you answered so confidently, I kind of got nervous and changed what I was going to say."

I'm gagged. "*You* were nervous?"

"Yeah, I actually recognised you as that cute guy who stopped the bank robbery, and I choked because you were even more cute and confident in real life."

"Oh . . . I see." My hands stop fidgeting, and I bring them up to lay on the table, almost speechless. It never occurred to me that someone could feel nervous about asking *me* out. It's always me that's the one pining and stressing over a guy.

"Are you okay?" he asks, reaching out his hand to brush his fingertips against mine.

"Yeah, actually, I am. Hey, can we just start fresh? I mean, I think I've proven now that I'm not some crazy-confident, intimidating guy," I say with self-deprecating chuckle.

"I think that sounds pretty good. Let's start right now. Come on, let's go somewhere more private," he says, grasping my hand and pushing his chair back to stand up.

"But she said we can't leave until it's over."

"Oh, don't worry about that. I know Cherry. We're friends. Under all that make up, glitter and dress, is a six-foot-one bear like me. Well *almost* like me, I'm six-four."

Jesus, it's like he's *trying* to make me melt. He's friends with a drag queen, describes himself as a bear – which means that he's hairy – and he's six-four. He literally couldn't be anymore my type!

"Okay then, sure! Let's go," I say, standing in tandem with him. He waves over to Cherry to signal we're leaving the circle, and she just gives him a cheeky wink back. In the corner of my eye, I see that my second date managed to swap his position. He's now on a table with some hunky dude, and it looks like they're getting on. Good for him.

"Can I buy you a drink?" Logan asks, pulling me to the bar.

"Yeah," I look up at him, smiling as I lose myself in his deep, maroon eyes. And don't worry, I watch the drink being made to ensure no funny business occurs.

TOO LATE?

We drink, chat, and dance the night away until we're both dripping with sweat. At least he won't judge me for my excessive sweating then. After a while, we head to the smoking area for some 'fresh' air.

"You know, you really didn't need to be nervous about asking me out when you're this hot." I playfully dance my fingers across his chest.

"Please, you're way sexier," he compliments me, placing his hand on my waist.

"Yeah, alright." I brush off with awkward laughter.

"Don't be like that."

"Like what?"

"Don't put yourself down. You're smoking hot," he says using the hand planted on my waist to pull me in closer to him. His body radiates heat, and the smell of his cologne is hypnotising. "You're amazing just the way you are," he says, quoting Bruno Mars, though I'm not sure if he realises that, or how cheesy it sounds. I don't care though, his cheesiness is cute, and his body is sexy. God, how am I supposed to resist him?

Simple, I don't.

I throw my arms around his thick neck and rest them over his broad shoulders. His hands grasp my waist even firmer as we instinctively pull in closer until our lips meet. We kiss passionately for at least a minute before we release each other, and he keeps hold of me, allowing my hands to slip down from his neck to his pecs.

"You know, my apartment is only two blocks away," Logan says, a suggestive glint in his eye.

As good as it feels to be wanted by such a godlike man, and as much as I'd love to jump his bones right now, I made a promise to myself not to. I don't want this to be another fuck-and-chuck, and if I sleep with him now, then that could be a possibility. *And* as much as I'd like to take credit for that mature epiphany, it was strongly helped along by Carmen's green eyes searing into the back of my head. Although, she's also busy necking off with some girl, so she's not exactly being a great role model herself.

Oh, and for anyone wondering why we were only swiping guys before – for one, don't, it's none of your business. Secondly, it's because Carmen swears that she'll settle down with a guy, despite being attracted to both. Though, I have a feeling that might change.

"Look, I know it sounds super cheesy, and it couldn't be any more ironic considering this club is pretty well known for people getting off in the toilets, but I'm not looking for another one-night stand," I coyly inform him, hoping he doesn't think I'm boring.

"That's not cheesy at all, though yes, a little ironic, I'll give you that. But you shouldn't change your morals for anyone and, for the record, I wasn't looking for a one-night stand with you, either. So, how about I take you on a date tomorrow instead?"

"Really? You seriously don't mind?" I ask, returning to my more chipper mood.

Ew. I can't believe I just described myself as 'chipper'. I'm really becoming a whole new person here, huh?

"Nope, I don't mind at all. I have a feeling that you'll definitely be worth the wait."

I can't help but smile uncontrollably, giving him another kiss before saying goodbye. He watches and laughs as I drag Carmen away from sucking some poor

TOO LATE?

girl's face off like a dementor from *Harry Potter*. I manage to get us back to the apartment, and let Carmen take half my bed as I head over to the bathroom and brush the alcoholic taste off my tongue and teeth. I open my mirror cabinet to see the usual collection of pills but, for the first time in a long time, I don't have the urge to pop every single bottle and chug them.

And *that* is a nice feeling to have.

CHAPTER 6

RELEARNING HAPPINESS

I wake up to the angelic sound of Carmen throwing up in my bathroom. I certainly won't be cleaning it up, though I still go to her aide by holding her hair back, because I'm not a *total* monster. I'm a little hungover myself, but nothing a bit of breakfast can't fix. Carmen, on the other hand, looks like she's just had the Devil exorcised out of her.

"How're you doing?" I ask, my enquiry met with more retches as she fills up my toilet bowl. The stench is vile to the point where my nostrils are burning, and she finally stops the demonic vomiting just long enough for me to flush. Sitting back, Carmen wipes her mouth with the back of her hand, leaving it coated in lovely chunks of sick.

"All done?" I ask, though it's really more of a threat than a question. She nods. "Awesome! I'm going to get dressed and sort Lucky out, and *you* can join me for breakfast when this sitch is dealt with." I gesture at the sicky bathroom, and she gives me a shaky thumbs-up in reply.

About an hour later, Carmen emerges from the bathroom looking good as new. I'm surprised, for a second, but then remember that this is what she does best. She could have been in a war zone last night, and she'd *still* have walked out of that bathroom looking red-carpet-ready.

"Sorry about earlier," she apologises casually.

"Oh, it's fine, it happens to everyone." I brush it off as if I'm not traumatised by the ordeal.

"What's for breakfast?" she asks.

I mean, I know I offered her some but, honestly, how can she be thinking of food after that performance?

"Er . . . pancakes?" I suggest.

"With bacon and maple syrup?" she asks, bearing puppy dog eyes that would give Lucky's a run for their money.

"Yeah, sure," I smirk.

"Thanks, kiddo."

I start making my signature, amazingly fluffy, buttermilk pancakes when Carmen notices that I'm wearing aftershave, and that I'm dressed up as if ready to go on another night out.

"Doing anything special today?" she inquires.

"Huh?" I turn to see her looking at me with one eyebrow raised. "Oh, you mean because of this?" I say, presenting my outfit. "Well, you remember that guy from last night?"

"The vet?"

"Yes, the vet. His name is Logan, and he asked me to go out with him today after I told him last night that I wasn't just looking for *fun*."

"Oh my God, yas queen! You think he might be boyfriend material?"

"I hope so, but we'll have to see how this date goes."

"I hope it goes well! You deserve to be happy, and it'll be such a good meet-cute! I mean, first he's your vet, and then you bump into each other at a speed dating night! What else do you need to happen before you realise it's destiny?" She describes it like some sort of princess fairytale.

"While I appreciate the enthusiasm, I don't think it's quite as cute as you're making it sound. I mean, you're missing out the part where he blew me off the first time I met him. Or the part where I called him a loser for being at a speed dating event."

"Oh, please, they're just semantics, which only make the story that much more relatable, not to mention adorable! But you really do deserve this," she smiles sweetly.

"Thanks, Carmen," I smile back.

I plate up two stacks of pancakes with a couple rashers of bacon on each and a generous glug of maple syrup. Somehow, Carmen, being the little pocket rocket that she is, manages to nail them in a minute without so much as a hiccup.

TOO LATE?

"You really are something else. Two hours ago, you were wrecked," I say, half impressed, and half worried that the pancakes might come back up at any moment.

"I know, it's a talent, isn't it? I just feel so *refreshed* after a night-out-throw-up-sesh," she says, with a deep calming breath in through her nose.

"I wish I could say the same. My head's all over the place, to be honest," I admit, still feeling a little groggy.

"We *did* get pretty wasted last night. It was fun, though. I've missed it. I feel like it's been ages since we've spent time together outside of work. When you were with Ben, we'd only ever hang out as a trio and then, when you broke up, you were always too down in the dumps to do anything."

"I know, I'm sorry that it took an armed robbery to wake me up to the fact that I need to spend more time with my bestie."

"It's okay," Carmen says, "I know you were going through a rough time, and I'm sorry if you felt like you couldn't talk to me about it."

She's right, I *did* feel like that, and a part of me still does – hence why I haven't told her about what really happened at the bank. *Should I tell her?* No, the doc said to start fresh. Which means I don't need to dwell on *that* anymore.

"You know you can tell me anything, right? I'm your Latina bisexual bestie, there's not much I can't handle," she kids, making me chuckle. "Seriously, is there anything you want to tell me?" she reiterates, almost as if she knows I'm hiding something.

"Nope, nothing to report at the moment," I lie.

"Okay . . . so, where are you going for this date?"

I'm unsure whether she's convinced by my answer, but I don't have time to ponder that right now as I realise that I don't have an answer to her question. Where *am* I going on this date?

"Oh, I don't know actually. I should probably message him. Oh, shit! I only gave him *my* number! I don't have his! Ugh, I bet he ghosts me now!" I say, sliding my phone across the breakfast bar in a huff.

In perfect timing, the breakfast bar vibrates, and the edges of my phone screen light up purple, signalling an *actual* text message – not a DM from one of my various forms of social media.

"That's probably him, check it!" Carmen demands, looking more excited than even I am.

"No, I'm too scared! You check it," I moan.

"Gladly." She grabs the phone, unlocking it with my password pattern, which I'm assuming I told her at some point and just forgot. Her eyes squint as she focuses on the screen. It doesn't help that she refuses to wear her prescription glasses.

"Well?" I blurt impatiently.

"He said he had a great time last night and can't wait to see you for dinner. He said he'll pick you up, and that he's got your address from work. That's so romantic," she beams, her tone sickly-sweet.

"I mean, it's a little stalker-y."

"Oh, shut up! He's really into you, dude!"

"I know! So, inevitably, I'm bound to mess it up!" I stress.

"Don't think like that. Just be yourself! He obviously likes your quirkiness so far."

That's easy for her to say.

TOO LATE?

"Yeah, but what about when he sees my, even more, batshit-crazy side?"

She laughs in response. "Brian, you're such a boob. Look, *que sera, sera*. Whatever will be, will be. But you don't need to change yourself for anyone! It's like those baby toys, you know the ones where each shape has a hole that it fits into? You're a unique shape, Brian, I'll give you that, but somewhere out there is an equally-as-unique hole that you'll fit with. Hopefully that's Logan, but if not, then don't worry! We'll find your hole I promise."

"I mean, that was an oddly sexual analogy but, thanks," I smile.

"Ew, dude, you know what I meant," she says pulling a face.

"*You* were the one talking about finding me the right hole, ya creep!" We both laugh.

"Right, I better go, and let you relax for a little while before he gets here."

"What are you talking about? We've only just had breakfast, we've got loads of time," I rebut, as I slide the dishes into the sink.

"Dude, we're hungover. Look at the actual time that we just had *breakfast*," she says pointing to my phone.

I look to see. "*Two!* Already?"

"Yep! We're old now, dude, we don't recover as fast."

"You're not kidding," I say, my face gawping.

"As I said, I best be going. I've got a shitload of errands to get done before we go back to work next week."

"Ugh, don't remind me of that horrid place."

"I'll see ya later," she chuckles, before giving me a syrupy kiss goodbye on the cheek and leaving.

"Bye," I call out from the sink scrubbing my now-sticky cheek.

***

I've spent the last couple of hours procrastinating about my date, and telling Lucky that the nice man from the vets will be her new daddy soon.
Mine too, hopefully.
Logan sends another message to say he'll be here at five. It's now twenty to five, so I use what precious time I have left to respray my pits – for the thousandth time today – and to make sure that there isn't a single hair on my head that's out of place. Hopefully the 'cool breeze'-scented antiperspirant will be enough to mask my anxiety sweats. I doubt it, though. Also, why is it called 'cool breeze'? It's a deodorant, not a car air-freshener.

The speaker to the building's front door rings. I answer and it's him! He's five minutes early – which I like, because I'd always rather be an hour early than five minutes late, so at least we have timekeeping in common. Jesus, I sound so boring right now! Who says timekeeping is something they have in common with a date? That's the kind of shit you say in an interview. Thankfully, he wasn't around for me to accidentally air that thought to.

"Hey." Logan's smooth-as-caramel voice carries through the speaker.

"Hi," I answer, trying not to sound as nervous as I am on the inside.

"Are you ready, or do you want me to come up and wait?"

TOO LATE?

"No! Er . . . I mean yes! I'm ready! I'll be down in a sec!" There is no way I'm letting him see my dumpy-ass apartment on the first date!

"Okay . . ." he replies, sounding confused.

I give Lucky a quick snuggle before heading down the communal stairs to see him stood on the other side of the glass door to the building. He is looking *fine*, and he hasn't noticed me yet because his back is to me. He's looking around, and probably checking out the crappy neighbourhood that I live in. He told me last night that he lives in Manhattan, so he's probably not used to roughing it. I sneak out of the door and tap on his shoulder from behind him.

"Hey."

"Oh hey! Wow . . . you look great!" he says, turning around and looking me up and down – in a nice way, not like a judgmental, mean-girl way.

"Thanks," I smile, my cheeks flushing. "So . . . where are we going?"

"Well, I thought I'd take you on the *ultimate* date," Logan says, taking my hands in his.

"Okay, I'm listening. What does that entail, exactly?"

"Food, drinks, bowling, crazy golf, arcade, and romantic walk."

"Damn, that really is a lot in one date."

"What can I say, I'm an ambitious guy," he smiles and God, he has such a cute, wholesome smile!

"Well, you're a vet, so I already assumed that," I point out.

"Yeah, I guess so," he chuckles.

"So, where to first?"

"Crazy golf?" he suggests, not yet knowing that my competitive spirit is fierce.

"Only if you're ready to lose, because I am a pro when it comes to crazy golf," I say with a bit of sass, easing more into being around him.

"Hmm, I think you're going to eat those words later," he retaliates, perfectly matching my cocky sportsmanship.

I wish I could eat him later.

He's so hot, and suave, and I still can't believe that *he* was the one nervous to ask *me* out! I guess even hot people get insecure. He seems a lot more comfortable now, though that's probably because he's already seen me when I'm drunk and at my worst.

"You're on!" I finally answer him.

"Let's go," he says, with an excitable smile across his face. Truly, I've only ever seen Lucky look that happy to see me, and she's only been my dog all of one week.

***

We play golf and, as I creep into the lead, I realise that I made a rookie mistake. I should've *pretended* to be bad. This could've been the perfect opportunity to have his big, hunky arms around me, as I fake being terrible at the task. I truly missed out on that one! And I can't do it when we go bowling. I can't pretend to be bad at *that*. You can't have two people throwing one bowling ball. That wouldn't look sexy, we'd just look like idiots.

"Wow, you actually beat me!" he almost shouts in disbelief as he finishes totting up the score card.

TOO LATE?

"I *did* warn you. Though, I'll admit, you were a very worthy adversary. You had me scared for a couple moments, especially when you got a hole-in-one twice," I say, twirling my golf club playfully.

"Yeah, well, I'm *definitely* going to beat you at bowling," he says, hooking my waist with his club and pulling me in for a kiss.

Fuck that was so cool, I think as our lips meet.

"You hungry?" he whispers, looking down at me as he pulls his luscious lips away from mine.

"Always," I joke – though not really, I *am* always hungry – making us both snigger. It's then that I notice the poor staff member stood to the side, who's been patiently awaiting us to return the equipment. We pass everything over, and Logan takes my hand.

"You like Italian food?"

"Yeah, I love it," I smile up at him.

"Great! I know this amazing little place," he says, enthused.

After a short car ride, we arrive outside of a quaint Italian restaurant, simply called Vincenzo's. It's super cute, and feels authentic. I order a carbonara, and Logan orders something that I can't quite pronounce. He does it amazingly, though. Almost a little *too* well.

"Are you Italian, or something?" I ask playfully once the waiter has left with our orders.

"Half, technically," he smiles.

"Oh, you are? I was only joking because of how well you pronounced . . ."

"Fettuccine al Pomodoro?"

"Yeah, that," I smirk, feeling a little embarrassed. "So, is it just food you can say in Italian?"

"*No, bellissimo, posso dire tante cose.*"

"Okay, so you're fluent! God, you must think I'm so boring seeing as I'm a one-hundred-percent redneck Texan." I look down, deflated.

"Brian," he says, tilting my chin up so my eyes are once again in line with his. "There is certainly nothing boring about you. Besides, my Italian may sound good to you, but to my Ma, it's too 'American-sounding'."

"Thanks." I place my hand on his.

"For what?" he asks, confused.

"Making me feel comfortable."

"You deserve to feel comfortable, wherever you go, but especially when I'm around," he smiles.

A few seconds of staring into each other's eyes later, and the food arrives. The waiter places the dishes in front of us and now that I can see what Logan's ordered, it looks delicious – almost as much as *he* does. We tuck in, but I can't help but keep looking over to his meal.

"Do you want to try some?" he asks, probably sensing my eyes watching him like a hawk.

"You don't mind?"

"Course not! Here," he offers, holding out his fork with some pasta wrapped around it.

Well, *this* is a new experience! Ben *never* shared his food, and if I ever asked to try some, he'd passively-aggressively fat-shame me. He had the perfect way of making me feel like crap without actually saying anything directly offensive so I couldn't warrant being upset with him. But Logan just keeps getting better and better. Maybe it's too good to be true?

"Wow, that tastes amazing!" I mumble, finishing the forkful he so cutely fed me.

TOO LATE?

"I can order another, if you want? Dinner is on me, anyway."

"I can pay half, there's no need for you to pay for everything," I offer feeling slightly insulted. *Does he not think I can afford it?*

"I really don't mind. I like you, and I'm happy to splurge a little on a date with you," he says. Maybe he thinks he's being cute, or my saviour, paying for me because I'm poor. It's only now just occurred to me that he paid for golf, too.

"I'm not a gold digger, you know? I know my apartment building isn't exactly The Ritz, but I'm not a charity case," I bark, my inner saboteur getting the better of me once again.

"Woah, where's all this coming from?"

"I saw you looking around outside my apartment, like you were gonna catch something by standing on the doormat."

"Brian, you've really got the wrong idea, and if you thought that, then why'd you even agree to go out with me in the first place? Oh, and for the record, I was looking around because I was trying to figure out where *my* childhood apartment was from there. I grew up in the same neighbourhood. And if you *were* a gold digger, you'd be a pretty shit one. You know I'm a vet, not a millionaire, right?"

He makes his point pretty well, and he has that same stern look on his face as when I messed up at the bar. Fuck! Why can't I just trust that *maybe* he's a nice guy? It was going so well! Why do I have to ruin everything? I gulp the anxiety-induced saliva that's been lingering in my mouth and prepare to apologise my ass off in the hopes that he doesn't think I'm totally crazy.

"I'm sorry," I start, "it's just that you're the first guy I've liked and gone on a date with in a long time, and I think my stupid brain was just searching for a reason to sabotage something that was going well. I'm sorry," I repeat.

He stretches out his long, husky arm across the table and gently tucks his hand beneath mine. "You're not stupid. Trust me, I understand how it feels to be insecure – I was fat as a kid."

"No!" I'm shocked! He's so hunky now!

"Yes," he chuckles at my over-the-top reaction. "But I also know that you need to allow yourself to be liked by others. Because I really like you, Brian. Even if you *do* put the *crazy* in crazy golf." We both laugh at that one. "*And* if you jump to wrong conclusions far too quickly." I look away feigning innocence. "Just give me a proper chance to show you who I am before you allow yourself to make another prediction about me, okay?"

"Yeah, okay. Sorry." I smirk coyly.

"You don't have to be sorry, you just have to pay half the bill because I changed my mind," Logan says with a cheesy grin on his face. He might be joking, but I do still want to pay half.

See, my dumbass insecurities were wrong yet again. Logan is *exactly* the guy I need. He's funny, sweet, understanding, and doesn't take himself too seriously. Oh, and just in case I hadn't mentioned it enough already, he is so hot! This is my second, or third, or possibly even *fourth* chance with him at this rate, but I need to make it my last!

TOO LATE?

Relax, Brian. Have fun. And don't fuck it up!

The rest of the date is a blast when I finally let my hair down and just have fun. We split the bill for dinner, but I graciously allow him to pay for bowling – and also let him win so he didn't feel too emasculated. Next, we spend all my change on the arcade games, and I beat him at every single one because I can't help it, I'm aggressively competitive, but I think he's into it.

We end up in one of those zombie-shooting video games that's in an enclosed capsule, shielded from the rest of the arcade. We both manage to get past the first level, with me bailing his ass out a few times, of course. By the second level, he's a goner, and he's surrounded by too many of the infected for me to revive him, so my character carries on in his memory. In the corner of my eye, I can see him watching me, rather than the screen as, eventually, I too am torn apart by flesh-eating zombies, I turn to face him.

"Hey," I say to break the silence.

"Hey," he says right back.

We shuffle a little closer together on the bench until we can stretch our necks so that our lips meet. The kiss envelopes us and, as it becomes more intense and fiery, he pulls my waist towards him, closing the remaining void of bench between us. The passionate moment comes to an abrupt, and aptly funny end, when my eyes flutter open for a split second, to see a zombie jumping out on the screen, causing me to shit myself and pull away.

"You were a pro at killing them a minute ago," Logan laughs, still gently holding my body in his hands.

"I can still be scared," I nudge him in his firm chest.

"Do you feel safer now?" he asks, once again pulling me in and wrapping his arms around me. I nod, biting my lip.

"You're so handsome," he says with ease, and I blush, not quite knowing how to respond. "I get the feeling you don't believe it yourself, but if I have to tell you every day until it sinks in, then I will."

"Can we go back to your place?" I ask, looking deeply into his maroon eyes.

"Are you sure? You don't have to," he reassures, caressing the small of my back.

"I don't think I've ever been surer about anything in my life."

"I want you so bad right now," he breathes heavily into my ear.

"Then let's go," I tease his lips with mine.

We exit the enclosed game to see a queue of ten-year-olds with evil eyes. I don't care because I'm on a high. One, because I'm about to go have the best sex of my life, and secondly, I just set a high score that those kids will go crazy trying to beat.

We get to Logan's apartment and out of excitement he fumbles his keys to open the door. We finally enter and, right away I can see that it's ten times nicer than mine. It's so modern and sleek – very much a bachelor pad. Suddenly, I'm greeted by the cutest little pug.

"Oh, this is Rex," Logan says, hanging our jackets up on a fancy, cast-iron coat rack. At my house, coats are tossed wherever. Usually on the floor.

"He's adorable!" I fawn over the dog.

"No, he's a grumpy little shit," Logan says, turning to see me on the floor, Rex licking my face. "Maybe *you*

TOO LATE?

should be a vet. If you can make *that* mopey beast love you, then you've definitely got what it takes."

"Thanks," I chuckle, giving Rex belly rubs.

"Do you want a drink?"

"No, thanks," I answer, getting up and waltzing over to him as I remind us both why I wanted to come over in the first place.

We start kissing, and Rex gets a little jealous, so Logan *picks me up* and carries me to his bedroom. Free from the puppy's prying eyes, he gently drops me onto the bed and starts undressing in front of me. He starts with his shirt, revealing his hairy puffed-out chest. He doesn't have defined abs but I couldn't care less, all I need is that chest, those arms, and a good back to cling onto – which he also has. I stand up before him and sensually run my fingers over his chest, allowing them to trickle down to his jeans.

Our lips touch as I tug at his jeans to free him of them, and I pull them down to see that he's wearing jersey-style boxers – my favourite type – the ones that allow everything to hang free. And, even though I prefer briefs on myself, because I like to keep everything in place at all times, I can't think of anything sexier for him to be wearing right now.

He starts to pitch a tent as I drop a kiss on his lower stomach, slowly edging closer to his manhood. I pull down his boxers to reveal *it*, his penis flicking up like a spring as it's finally released from its cage. I kiss the base of it before running my tongue along the shaft, allowing my mouth to be filled by the humbling, large-enough, seven-inch penis. As I work my magic on him, his eyes roll into the back of his head.

Told you I was good.

After a minute, he gently stops me, pulling me into a standing position. I've remained dressed until this point because I'm scared that he won't approve of what's beneath my clothes. He goes to pull up my shirt and I nudge it back down with my hands, trying not to show the fear on my face.

"Please, trust me," he whispers into my ear, and I decide to take the doc's advice – fake it till I make it.

I nod, allowing him to remove my shirt. He then pulls down my trousers and briefs, placing his hands on my waist and standing back for a second to take a good look at everything while my head remains tilted down. I'm too scared to look up and see whatever facial expression is now sprawled across his face, but he places his forefinger under my chin and lifts my face up to see his.

"You are perfect," he whispers. I let out a little smile of approval, and, with that, he picks me up so that my legs wrap around his waist and my arms are around his neck and shoulders. He has my bum firm within his grasp, and feeling his naked skin against mine sends a euphoric sensation down my spine. He tells me I'm beautiful as he says, "do you still want to–"

I place my finger on his lips and answer. "Yes."

"You finally cut me off to answer the right question," he chuckles, still holding my entire body weight without so much as a tremble. Then, he takes me to the bed and makes love to me all through the night. I'm a bottom and he's a top so we fit together perfectly and, what makes it even *more* delectable, is that he's a *generous* top,

TOO LATE?

reciprocating the oral pleasure that I had already shown him.

I fall asleep snuggled up in his arms, but the next morning he has to leave early for work. Unlike Ben, who would've kicked me out at six a.m., Logan softly wakes me with a shower of kisses to explain that he has to go to work, but also says that I can stay for as long as I want. He even mentions that he'd be extremely happy if I was still here when he got back. I thought it was a dream at first, as I was still half asleep when he said it. But, when I fully wake up at around eight-thirty to Rex licking my face, I see a little post-it note stuck to a key on the bedside table. It reads:

Morning, handsome!

There's some bacon and bagels in. Help yourself, and hopefully I'll see you later.

X Logan X

You know, I think I'm finally remembering how it feels to be happy. I haven't experienced it a whole lot in my life, but *this* . . . this is definitely it.

CHAPTER 7

THE FINAL SESSION

Three months later

"Brenda, I'm telling you, I don't need them anymore. I promise, I'm doing great now. I have a boyfriend, friends, career prospects and I'm actually *happy*," I stress to her.

"Brian, it's not that simple."

What does *she* know anyway? She's just a glorified agony aunt!

Sorry I've not been around for the last few months. I'm sure you're wondering what's happened, so I guess it's time for another 'previously on'.

Last time you saw me, I was waking up in Logan's apartment to that cute post-it note that made me feel all

TOO LATE?

fuzzy inside. I did indeed stay and wait for him to return home, where I cooked him a meal and we had another night of hot, passionate love-making. Oh, and don't worry, Carmen looked after Lucky for the day, I'm a good dog dad.

Since then, we've moved in together – or rather, Lucky and I moved into his place. Because, let's be honest, it was a damn sight fancier than mine. The dogs surprisingly get along just as well as we do. Lucky can definitely hold her own against Rex, and they've adopted a cute little brother-sister relationship with not a single humping sesh in sight.

Logan and I both said "I love you" last week. I knew way before that, but I didn't want to scare him off by being too forward. And that's pretty much it, regarding the love life – we're quite the happy little family unit.

As for work, after not finding any jobs that remotely interested me, Logan managed to convince me to go into his career. It started off as a joke, because of how good I was around Rex when I first met him but, the more I thought about it, the more excited I got. I love animals – way more than humans, anyway – and I was actually quite the academic genius in high school, believe it or not, I just never had the opportunity to apply for college – what with being kicked out for being a gay pariah, and all.

But *now*, I have a stable home and a supportive boyfriend. So, I finally got to do what I've always wanted, which was to waltz into ABA Bank and tell Susan that she can shove her job right up her . . . well, you know what. Now I'm enrolled in college, studying to become a vet and, in the meantime, I'm helping Anne out on reception. It means that I'm still making a bit of money for myself, and I get some hands-on experience. Plus, when Anne's not there, I get to be in control of the drugs.

So, as I was saying to Brenda, life is pretty awesome right now, and I don't need to be on the happy pills anymore – but she just won't listen to me.

"Brian, you can't just *stop* taking them. We can talk about easing you off them, but to go cold turkey is extremely dangerous. You could experience major mood swings that might throw you into a depressive state and make you vulnerable again."

"Well, I already stopped a few days ago and I feel fine," I snap back.

"You did *what*? Brian, the effects might not manifest right away, but they could still hit you soon. I promise, I'm only trying to look out for you. I'm going to prescribe you another box, and I want you to take them every other day. We'll see how that goes, okay?"

"Nah, I'm good," I stand up, readying to leave. "Oh, and this will be our last session. I appreciate everything, Doc, but my life is on track now, and I need to start living it. Besides, I'm sure I'll find something better to spend one hundred and fifty dollars an hour on," I say walking out.

I know that sounded mean, but she just wasn't taking the hint.

"But, Brian! Wait!" Brenda shouts to an already-closed door.

I leave the building and let out a sigh of relief, knowing that I've unofficially graduated therapy – at least by my standards, anyway. Oh! You'll probably be wanting an update on Carmen, too!

TOO LATE?

She's also doing good. Like me, she managed to get out of that horrid bank. She's actually got a job working with an LGBTQ+ charity now, helping the new generation of queers. She's away a lot doing great work, so I don't get to see as much of her anymore, but I'm so proud of her – and now I have Logan, so I don't mind.

Carmen's also got a girlfriend now. I know, right! Told you she'd end up settling down with a girl. I could feel it. Her name's Cynthia and they're really cute together, and we're actually all getting together tomorrow night at our place for a dinner party that Logan and I are hosting. I honestly can't wait to take a break from studying to just eat, drink, and play games with my friends.

I know. I said "friends".

As in *plural*.

It's kinda weird saying it out loud. For so long it was just me and Carmen, but now look at me – hosting dinner parties like a proper adult! Logan's friend is also coming. You remember Cherry Cola from speed dating, right? It's him. His real name is James.

James is really kind, and I probably see him more than Carmen lately. He's been dating someone for the past month, and we've all been eager to meet them. And so, after much begging, he's finally bringing his new partner along. They're called Jo and they're non-binary. From what James has told us about them, they seem just as adorably sweet as he is, and I'm super excited for us all to get together. Anyhow, I've got to go to the grocery store and buy all of the ingredients for tomorrow.

***

I'm perusing the vegetable aisle for some Jerusalem artichoke – I know, *fancy* – when I spot Ben at the opposite end. Now that I have a real boyfriend to brag about, I'm not scared of bumping into him. In fact, I think I'll *bump* into him right now! I push my cart down the aisle until I *accidentally* crash into his, quickly looking away and then back to the carts as though it was a complete accident.

"Oh, *hi*!" I greet him very chipper, feigning surprise.

"Hey," he sounds a little solemn.

"How are you?" I ask first, to assert my confidence because, let's be honest, everyone knows that you only really ask that first because then the other person has to ask you the same question back, out of politeness. That's when you get to decimate them with your amazing news.

"Er, been better. Joel and I . . ." *I assume that's his slutty twink boyfriend,* "are going through a bit of a rough patch at the moment, but I'm sure we'll get through it," he says looking genuinely sad.

"Aw, that's awful news. But yeah, you're right, I'm sure you'll make up soon," I reassure him, so that he'll be emotionally stable enough to ask me the same question back.

"How are yo–" he begins to ask.

"Oh, *me*? I suppose I'm doing okay. I mean, I *do* have an amazing boyfriend, and we do live together in Manhattan. He's a vet, did I mention? Oh, and I'm also training to become a vet, too. We'll probably open up our own practice one day. So, I guess you could say life is pretty great at the moment!"

That felt so good. I have officially won the breakup. I know it might seem a little late to say that, but need I

TOO LATE?

remind you of the fable of the tortoise and the hare? Bitch, I'm the motherfucking tortoise!

"That sounds great, but you know you don't need to impress me, right?" Ben seems unphased by my amazing brag. Why isn't he breaking down and sobbing where he stands? Why isn't he distraught that I'm winning the breakup? Does he not understand the rules? Do I need to spell it out?

"Impress you? What are you talking about? I'm just trying to live my best life," I *smize* at him.

"If you were truly living your *best* life, then you wouldn't have spotted me from across the store and charged your cart at me. It's coming across as a little desperate, honestly, especially when we both know your new life is based on a lie," he says, rather spitefully.

"What are you babbling on about?"

"Look, I don't know exactly what happened in the bank that day, but I *do* know, for a fact, that Brian Christian is no hero. The Brian *I* know, would have never risked his own life for some strangers. Because, even if you weren't a selfish bitch, you'd still be too chicken to do anything about it," Ben spits.

"What the hell, Ben? Why are you being like this?"

"Because this isn't *you*! You're pretending to be someone you're not! And I think that Carmen, and your new *boyfriend*, deserve to know the truth!"

"The *truth* is that I saved the day and you're just jealous because I've moved on and your life has gone to shit."

"If that's what you want to think."

"It's what I *know*."

"Listen, if you can live with lying to the people that you love for the rest of your life, then go ahead and enjoy all the guilt that will ensue. I hope it eats you from the inside out."

"Oh, fuck off! You've always been a toxic piece of shit, Ben, and you're one to talk about *lying*! You cheated on me for *months*, you hypocrite! I don't need to take this from you anymore, because *I'm* not the one sucking your tiny cock! I hope that poor *Joel* sees some sense and dumps your ass!"

Who does he think he is, anyway? He can't judge *me* after everything *he* did! And now, I see that all of that spiel in the park was exactly that – rotten spiel. I can't believe he's still trying to make me miserable, even when he isn't a part of my life anymore. Well, I'm not going to let his jealousy affect me. No, fuck that! Fuck him! And fuck Brenda too, while we're at it! I'm sick of everyone telling me how I should live my life!

Now, I've got a pissing dinner party to plan! So, excuse me as I storm over to the checkout and pay for my groceries before racing home in anger. Yes, I'm driving now, do you have a problem with that? Yes, Logan helped me with a down payment, but *I'm* paying the rest, and he did that because he's a good boyfriend, unlike Ben!

***

The next morning, I begin preparing everything for dinner. Logan enters the kitchen, giving me a kiss and squeeze before he gets ready to leave for work.

"Make sure you're back in time to wash up before dinner," I remind him.

TOO LATE?

"I thought you found my scrubs sexy?" he smoulders at me with a raised eyebrow.

"Yeah, I do . . . when they're *clean*. I've seen your schedule today, and it's one castration after another. I don't want the smell of sweaty dog testicles stinking up our dinner party."

"Ever the way with words, my love, but I see your point. I'll make sure I'm home early," he smiles, swaggering over to give me another kiss.

"Thank you," I manage to say, just before he plants one on me.

"See ya later," he waves, heading out the door.

"Bye!"

I spend most of the day preparing the meal, making sure that I take a well-deserved lunch break to *try* all of said dishes and catch up on some television. In reality, I'm watching *Friends* for the umpteenth time and, although I should be laughing at Joey, or trying to decide what percent of Rachel, Monica, and Phoebe make up my personality – I can't.

I have this feeling niggling in the back of my mind, and I recognise it as Ben's words, repeating over and over again, telling me how I'm lying to the people I love. I know he said those things out of spite, but some of it *was* true. They *do* deserve to know the truth. And it's not that I *want* to lie to them, I just don't know how to tell them.

I've been lying to Carmen since it happened, and I've been lying to Logan since we met. What if they both think what I did is unforgiveable and they . . .

No! I don't want to think about it! I just need to keep it up! I'm in too deep now, and telling them would only ruin everything for everyone.

***

It's later in the day, and Logan arrives mere minutes before we're expecting our guests. I playfully smack him on the butt and tell him to hurry up and get ready. Of course, he's all cute and apologetic. A few minutes later, as I finish laying the table, the speaker buzzer rings. It's Carmen and Cynthia. I buzz them up, and wait by the door.

"Hey!"

"Hi," they reply in tandem.

"Nice place," Cynthia compliments.

"Thanks! It's about time we had you guys over. As delicious as your cooking is, Cynthia, I thought that it was about time that Logan and I put some effort in and hosted *you*."

"Girl, you don't understand how glad I am that you guys are hosting tonight. You know whenever *we* host, it's actually *me* who does everything! Carmen just walks around looking pretty," Cynthia laughs.

"I can certainly believe that! I'd say I have the same situation, but Logan was in work today so I can't be mad at him for that . . . I guess," I chuckle.

"You know, at first I was glad that you guys got along, but now it feels like a constant dump-on-Carmen fest," Carmen jokes, to which Cynthia and I laugh, rolling our eyes.

"Come on in, guys. Take a seat, and I'll bring a bottle of wine over."

"Thanks," they both smile as they choose a seat at the table.

TOO LATE?

Eventually, Logan appears from the bedroom looking very suave in his navy turtleneck. It's slim fit, so I'll be ogling him all night.

"Hey, everything ready?" he asks, planting a kiss on my cheek.

"Yeah, we're just waiting on James and Jo."

"Awesome, I'm sure they'll be here any sec–" the speaker buzzer rings again. "I guess that'll be them! I'll buzz them up."

"Okay."

When everyone's seated, I serve up the starters – carrot and sweet potato soup. We're all mostly getting to know Jo, with them being the newest member of our group. They seem like the perfect match for James, and the pair of them make a rather similar-looking couple to me and Logan, to be honest. I'm sure, in time, Jo and I will be able to gas about our hunky partners.

The rest of dinner goes down a treat, as everyone loved my roasted duck with a red wine jus and mixed roasted veggies, and don't even get me started on dessert. I made Logan's favourite, his mom's famous tiramisu recipe. Turns out it was a fan favourite all round, as everyone wanted a second helping.

We move on to some games, which of course brings out my competitive side. Despite that, we're all having fun until Jo asks me a question during an intense game of Cluedo.

"Hey, Brian, I feel like I recognise you. Have we met before? Or are you like, *famous*, or something?"

James answers for me. "Oh, I *completely* forgot to tell you! Brian here is our in-house hero! Brian and Carmen worked at that bank that got robbed a few months back.

He's the guy that saved the day. It was all over the news at the time, so that's probably where you've seen him."

"Oh yes! Of course! I'm sure you're probably sick of talking about it by now, but that's incredible!" Jo smiles innocently, but I can't help but feel like, after Ben's lecture yesterday, this is just salt in the wound. It's not their fault, though. They don't know how painful it is to be reminded of the lie that I'm harbouring.

"Thanks," I reply coyly.

I just can't do this anymore. I can't relive this guilt every time someone brings it up. And it's not exactly something forgettable that might fade away over time. It was a *televised* event that is ingrained into local history. *My lies,* ingrained into local history.

I get up abruptly and head to the bathroom to hide the fact that I'm about to bawl my eyes out. I really don't want to tell them, but I can't keep living with this guilt anymore. I'm just so scared. For all I know, Logan wouldn't even *be* with me right now if I hadn't been branded a hero.

Catching a glimpse of myself in the bathroom mirror, I see that my eyes are red-raw and puffy, and my cheeks and neck are drenched in tears. I try to compose myself, but it's no use. I don't know how to make sense of anything anymore. I don't know what I should do. Maybe I should just . . . I hear footsteps just outside the door.

"Hey, you alright?" Logan asks. His usual caring self.

"Yeah," I reply, my voice shaky and unconvincing.

"Brian, I can hear that you're not okay. What's wrong? You know you can talk to me about anything."

I know I *can* talk to him, but I don't think I can bear to. Not yet. Not about this.

TOO LATE?

"Can you get Carmen?" I say.

"Oh, okay. Yeah sure. I love you," he says, the hurt showing in his voice.

"I love you, too," I whisper weakly, probably not loud enough for him to hear.

A few seconds later, Carmen's voice calls through the door and I unlock it to let her in.

"What's up, kiddo?" she asks as she sees the state of my face.

The worried look on her face makes the guilt feel even worse, which I didn't even think was possible. It's eating away at my insides – and there's not even the benefit of weight loss that you'd get from a physical parasite, like a tapeworm. No, I'm lumbered with something much worse, something that is all made up in my brain. Yet, it can make me feel like I've been stabbed in the stomach over and over.

It's time to release that pain.

It's time to tell the truth.

"I've been lying to you, Carmen. Logan, too. I never intended to, it just sort of . . . happened, and then I felt like I couldn't correct it because you'd all be ashamed or embarrassed by me. Or maybe you wouldn't even want to talk to me anymore," I ramble, my arms flailing.

"Brian, that's crazy talk. There's nothing you can do that would ever make me abandon you. We're a chosen family, and I chose you just as much as you chose me," she reassures me, clutching my shaky hands within hers and holding them to her mouth to kiss.

"Promise me you won't hate me."

"Done."

"No, say it! Please!" I make her swear.

"Brian, I promise! Whatever you're about to tell me, I won't hate you for it," she says, unfolding our hands to lock our pinkies together.

"Okay . . ." I take in a deep breath that burns my lungs, and exhale as I begin to explain myself. "You know the day of the robbery?"

"Yeah?"

"Well, I wasn't being some courageous hero. I genuinely *wanted* them to shoot me. I *wanted* to die! That's why I started off so quietly. It's only when they got loud about it that the perspective changed, and it looked like I was standing up to them. But I wasn't! It was just luck that everything played out the way it did. I'm so sorry I lied to you, Carmen. I feel bad enough about lying to Logan, but I should *never* have lied to you! You're my longest and best friend, and you've helped me through hardship before. I guess I just . . . didn't want to burden you again. I'm sorry. I'm just so sorry!"

I watch and wait for Carmen's face to react, as it currently looks vacant – and somewhat scared. She dips her head and sighs, clearly ashamed of me. I would be, too, if I were her. I wouldn't blame her if she wanted nothing more to do with me.

"I know, Brian," she mutters, her head still sunken between her shoulders.

"Know what?" I'm confused.

"That you wanted to kill yourself. I heard those first few whispers, and I knew they weren't for anyone else's benefit or spectacle. I knew you were looking for a way out. I convinced myself that it wasn't real, or that I misheard, or that you'd just . . . be okay. I buried my head

TOO LATE?

in the sand about it. Forgot about it. Ignored it. And I'm *so* sorry I did that, Brian!

"I should've been there for you! I should've confronted you about how you were feeling! For all I know, you could still be feeling that way now! I'm sorry I haven't been a better friend, and I'm sorry that you didn't feel you could talk to me about it until now. I'm just so sorry I let you down. But, Brian, you've *always* been my hero! I didn't need you to be some saviour. You're my best friend and, quite frankly, I don't know what I'd do without you! And I know this is an unquantifiable amount easier for me to say than it is for you to do, but *please,* don't ever try anything like that again! I love you, and I need you! So, if you're ever feeling alone in the world, or like no one cares, you pick up that damn phone and you call me! And I'll work harder to pick up on the signs, I promise! Plus, you've got that hunk out there now and, *my god* – he would move heaven and earth for you, Brian!"

"But I lied to him, too!"

"Then tell him the truth! He loves you deeply. I can see it in the way he looks at you – it's the same way *I* look at you. Now, before I send him in here, do you forgive me for being an awful friend?" she asks, her eyes barely able to keep contact with mine.

"Of course I do! Do you forgive me for the lies?" I request back.

"Already forgotten." Carmen smiles, holding out her arms as I leap into them.

I let my tears flow, and I pull away to see I've left a massive wet patch on her chest. "Sorry," I giggle.

"It's alright," she chuckles. "Are you ready for Logan now?"

I exhale. "Yes."

Carmen places a kiss on my forehead before trading places with Logan, and he kneels in front of my still-crying face. The faucet behind my eyes seems to be broken, and doesn't want to turn off.

"Brian, please tell me what's wrong," Logan says, wiping away my tears with his hand. I lean my cheek into his palm, his strength giving me the power to confess my truth once again.

"I've been lying to you," I whisper.

"About wha–"

"Please, just let me get it all out, and then you can say if you hate me, or whatever, at the end."

I can see him about to say, "I won't hate you," but I gently press my finger to his tender lips and carry on.

"I'm not a hero, and I'm not brave, Logan. I didn't purposely save anyone that day at the bank. I'd been struggling a lot with my mental health, to the point where I wanted to end my life, but I was too chicken to do it myself. So, the day of the robbery, I saw the perfect opportunity to pass on the burden to someone else.

"You see, it wasn't a public display of bravery, it was a private plea of cowardice to end my life. I know, since the day we met, that you thought I was this amazing person because of the news headlines, but I shouldn't have played along with it, and I definitely shouldn't have let *you* believe it!

"So . . . now you know. I'm selfish, and pathetic, and I hate myself for many reasons. But the biggest one of all is for lying to *you*! I'm sorry, Logan. I understand if you want me to move out, or if you hate me and never want to see me again."

TOO LATE?

"I–" he begins to speak, but I'm too nervous to listen to a reply so I interrupt him, as usual.

"I know you want nothing to do with me! I'll–" he stops me in my tracks by covering my mouth with his hand.

"What did we say about you finishing and answering my own questions?" he says, with a stern but comforting look, as he slowly takes his hand away.

"Sorry," I stay silent and hear him out.

"Brian Christian. I love you with all my heart! And though it does hurt to know that you kept something so important from me, it doesn't change the way I *feel* about you! And it doesn't change the person that *I* know you are! You're kind, loving, brave, hilariously funny, a tiny bit crazy," he chuckles, "and *my* boyfriend."

"How am I brave?" I ask, in incredible disbelief.

"At eighteen, your homophobic mother shunned you out of the house. You could've given up there and then, but you didn't. Instead, you moved hundreds of miles away, to New York, to start a new life for yourself, all alone! *That's* brave. You quit your job at the bank to pursue an actual career that you're passionate about. *That's* brave. You asked me out on the very first instance that we met. *That's* brave!

"You show your love for me, Carmen, Lucky, and Rex on a daily basis without holding back. *That's* brave. You wear socks and sandals at the beach, even though you know the extremely judgy gay guys will be there – and that's *hella* brave!" He gets a chuckle out of me for that one. "But most of all, you just told me the biggest secret you have. You didn't know how I was going to react, and you could've let it stay hidden away in the shadows, but you didn't. You chose to share that truth with me, and that's the bravest thing you could ever do.

"Brian, you *are* the bravest, most wonderful person I know, and whether the rest of the world thinks you're a hero or not, I'm proud to be your boyfriend. You ain't getting rid of me that easy."

"Promise?"

"I promise." Logan pulls me in for a hug and kisses my forehead. "Now, I know you said this was all way back at the bank but, do you still have *those* feelings now?" he asks, looking rightfully concerned.

"I'm so much happier now," I say, "especially now that I have you. But . . . I don't know. Sometimes I think there will always be a part of me that's a little anxious and depressive." This is dampening the mood further, but at least I'm being honest.

"Well, I promise I'll do anything and everything that I can to help. I don't want you to ever get to that point again. Do we need to get you a therapist, or do you already have one?"

It's honestly adorable that he cares so much. *God, I love him.*

Oh shit – my therapist!

"Er . . . I *may* have quit therapy, like, yesterday. But I'll call her tomorrow and go back! I thought I was ready to be *normal* again, but clearly not."

"There's absolutely *nothing* normal about you, and that's exactly why I love you. But if you need a bit more help on the road to feeling better, don't, for a second, think that there's anything wrong with that. And hey, if you need a personal cheerleader, I *will* buy an outfit," he smirks.

TOO LATE?

"That sounds pretty hot," I grin.

Logan rolls his eyes and scoops me into his muscular arms, my legs wrapping around his waist, and we just sit there on the bathroom floor, our bodies entangled.

"Are we okay?" he looks up at me.

I smile, nodding my head before meeting his lips with my own.

"I love you so much," I whisper as our lips part.

"I love you, too." His eyes are still closed. "Now, what do you say we team up and show those bitches out there who the Monopoly kings are?"

"Okay, sure, but you know I don't actually agree with the idea of a Monopoly market in the business place," I say, slipping back into my usual sassy self.

"Then why are you so damn good at it?" We both laugh.

He releases me from his loving grip, and I give my face a quick rinse with some cold water to reduce the puffy redness before we head back in to join a night of fun and games with my chosen family.

***

By eleven, everyone gets ready to head home. Logan and I are exhausted, and decide to leave the tidying up for our future selves in the morning. We don't make love, but simply rejoice in how blessed we are to be alive and in each other's arms. I snuggle up to his hairy chest, falling asleep with a smile on my face, as I know that now, with everything out in the open, I have a true second chance at life.

As I drift further into a deep slumber, I start to dream. In the dream, I'm in my old apartment, but it's empty now. There's no one to be seen or heard but, as I wander over to my old nemesis – the bathroom cabinet mirror – I come face-to-face with my reflection.

At first, nothing seems out of the ordinary as I open the cabinet and, it too, is empty. But, as I close it again, my reflection isn't there. A second later, my face reappears, scaring the life out of me. Only . . . it's not me. I mean, it's *me*, but it's not *my* reflection. The face in the mirror is moving of its own volition.

"Hello, Brian," the reflection speaks.

"Er . . . hi?" I reply, naturally a little spooked.

"Why are you still lying, Brian?" the reflection asks me.

"I'm not! I've told them now! They all know the truth, and they're okay with it! I'm happy now!" I answer to what I can only assume is my subconscious self.

"No, Brian. When are you going to stop lying to *yourself?*"

"What do you mean?" I knew I shouldn't have eaten all that cheese and chocolate. They say it gives you nightmares.

"*This*," Reflection Brian says, gesturing his arms around. "None of this is real!"

"I really don't understand what you're talking about! If this is supposed to be some "insecurity dream", can we just go back to the classic teeth-falling-out or being-naked-in-school scenarios? Those would be much less disturbing than whatever *this* is. I mean, I spent a lot of time in high school naked, anyway, if you know what I mean." Insert wink here.

TOO LATE?

"Would you just stop joking around. You're dead, Brian! God dammit!"

"Don't be ridiculous," I roll my eyes at this imposter.

"Brian!" the reflection shouts as I turn to walk away.

I head to my bedroom window and try to rid myself of these awful lies. I look outside, and all I see is a vast, white landscape. No dodgy neighbourhood. No druggies standing on the block corner.

Nothing.

As my gaze drops to the windowsill, Reflection Brian shows up again faintly in the glass of the bedroom window.

"Brian," he begins softly. "I'm sorry. The robber at the bank didn't miss. There was no warning shot – just the one that flew straight between your eyes. You're dead, Brian."

"No, no! That's not true! You're lying!" I shout back at the window in one last hurrah against what, deep down, a part of me already knows to be true and has known all along.

"I'm sorry, but yes. Yes, it is true. Everything since that moment has just been your brain trying to cope. Trying to make you feel better about what happened. Creating this world, so that death doesn't come so quickly or seem so scary. I'm sorry, Brian, but you . . . *me* . . . we're already gone. And now, it's time to pass on." He speaks calmly, and I know his words are true.

"But . . . I don't want to go," I plea. "My life is *good* now! I have a nice apartment, a new dog, career prospects, friends, a boyfriend! I finally have a family, and I'm truly happy for the first time in my life! I know

I'm not perfect, and I still have a long way to go but, for the first time in forever, I can finally see a path forward!"

I start to bawl. "I take it all back! I don't want to die! I don't want to kill myself anymore! Please, tell me there's something you can do?" I'm ironically pleading with myself.

"I'm sorry, Brian, but as I said, I'm you. There's nothing that can change this now. What's done is done. It's too late."

My whole world is crumbling around me.

For some godforsaken reason, my sick, twisted brain has given me a taste of what my life *could've* been like. My reflection describes it as a way of making death easier, but all it's done, is show me the life that I *could've* had! I know deep down this is my own doing! I didn't allow myself to have a second chance! I wished that away when I asked that robber to kill me. I may not have been the one to pull the trigger myself but, one way or another, I committed suicide, and it's too late for me now.

Please, if you're reading this, and you feel the same way – don't let it be too late for you, too.

EPILOGUE

BRIAN'S FUNERAL

Carmen Alverez was a wreck. She had just watched the last breath leave Brian's body as he hit the ground beside her. Shortly after that, the perpetrators turned to her asking for the money and, not wanting to meet the same fate as her best friend, she complied.

They were rough with her, grabbing her arms so tightly that, even a week on, she would still be bruised. But, in that moment, it wasn't the physical pain that hurt her – it was the fact that she'd complied with their orders while Brian laid next to her, lifeless. As soon as the robbers made their escape, police sirens emerged, making it to the scene in time to arrest the bastards responsible.

Carmen dropped to her knees and stroked Brian's cheek with the back of her hand. In the blink of an eye, she'd lost her best friend.

***

In the days after Brian's death, Carmen had been contacted by numerous reporters and news channels, but she'd been too distraught to face them, and hadn't known what she was supposed to say or do. It wasn't her place. It wasn't her story to tell. And so, as they do, the reporters created a story of their own, feeding off information from other witnesses. They called Brian a hero, and Carmen allowed him to be remembered in that way. To her, he *was* a hero.

Carmen had overheard the whispered discussion between Brian and one of the masked perpetrators. He'd wanted to die, and it had broken her heart to hear it. Carmen couldn't help but think that it was partly her fault.

How could she not?

She had been Brian's only friend, and she had seen some of the signs but had chosen to ignore them. She'd let him down, and so, in her eyes, the funeral would be her last chance to make it up to him – not that she ever *truly* could.

***

Carmen spent the following week making arrangements. She didn't have much choice in the matter, as there was no one else to do so. His parents had officially disowned

TOO LATE?

him not long after they kicked him out, and he didn't really have any other friends. Thus, Carmen planned a funeral for one guest.

***

The morning of the funeral, Carmen had just finished getting ready as the jet-black Mercedes arrived outside of her apartment building. She descended the stairs and sat in the back of the car as they followed the hearse. Barely keeping it together, her eyes stayed glued to her best friend's coffin ahead of her, and the ten-minute drive felt like an eternity. Something which Carmen assumed the rest of her life would feel like now without Brian around.

Once she arrived, she headed straight to the burial plot. At first, she was alone with the coffin, and the wreath of flowers beside it that spelled out BESTIE. But, not long after they started lowering the coffin, a few more people showed up, and gathered around to watch as Brian's body was laid to rest. Carmen didn't recognise most of the people around her. She assumed they knew Brian somehow, or perhaps they had heard the news and just wanted to pay their respects. There were a few people she definitely *did* recognise, though. The first of which, was Mr Fredrickson – one of their annoying regulars at the bank.

"Mr Fredrickson, what are you doing here?"

"I'm here to pay my respects to Brian. I know we didn't always see eye to eye, and I know I'm quite the grumpy old fogie but, the truth is, coming to the bank, and seeing you two – as good or bad as the interaction might've been – was always the highlight of my week."

"Oh wow . . . Mr Fredrickson . . . we had no clue you felt that way! I'm sorry for all those times I sassed you," Carmen chuckled.

"It's quite alright, dear," he smiled.

"No! No, it's not! If . . . *this* . . . has taught me anything, it's that life is too short, and we're not meant to be alone in it. Give me your phone," she politely demanded with her Latin charm. Mr Fredrickson pulled out a phone that looked so old, Carmen wasn't sure if she'd be able to work it.

"What do you want it for?" he asked as he gave it to her.

"I'm putting my phone number in, so if you ever feel lonely, or want to talk, or meet up for a coffee, we can," she explained, thumbing her number into his phone.

"Oh, thank you, Carmen. That means a lot."

"You're wel–" Carmen was about to finish her sentence, when her whole body filled with anger and disgust.

Brian's father was there.

She only knew his face from old pictures of Brian's, who had always held out hope that, one day, his father would see sense.

What Brian didn't know, was that his father, the night before Brian's death, had left his mother. He'd finally stood up to the intolerant wretch of a woman, and decided that a relationship with his son was worth a thousand times more than the one he endured with her. That night, he packed a bag and left. He finally replied to Brian's goodnight message after years of ignoring them.

TOO LATE?

He explained everything, and said that he was on his way to New York to make things right. Unfortunately, though, through twisted fate, Brian's phone had died the night before, and only finally charged at work when the robbers had arrived. Brian never got to see the message that could've tipped the scales on that fateful day.

"Sorry, Mr Fredrickson, would you excuse me for a moment?" Carmen said.

"Of course, dear, and please – call me Fred," he smiled, and she managed to glance one back at him before she strode over to the ignorant man that was Brian's father.

"You have some nerve showing up here," she kept her anger to a muted tone, out of respect for the situation.

"You must be Brian's friend," he replied calmly.

"No, I'm his family! What are you even doing here, anyway? He told me all about you – and *her*," Carmen scowled.

"I understand, and I'm not here to cause any trouble. I've left her," he said, as if it warranted an applause.

"Fucking congratulations! Shame it was five years too late!" Carmen spat.

"I was on my way to make things up to Brian when I heard about his death," he replied.

"*Make things up*? You didn't just ground him! You threw him out of his home for being *gay*! And then ignored him for *five years*!"

"Don't you think I know that? I've spent every day of the last five years regretting that!" he barked back, his eyes welling up. He stopped for a moment and allowed his voice to quieten once more. "And now . . . it's too late. My precious boy is . . . gone. I'm just glad they caught who did this," he blubbered, soaking up the tears with the cuffs of his suit.

"You think those idiots at the bank are the reason he's dead?" Carmen fumed. "You're more ignorant than I could ever have imagined! All *they* did, was what Brian asked of them. He felt so miserable and unworthy of living, that he asked strangers with guns to *kill him!*

"I take responsibility for not doing as much as I should've, trust me, I do. But you better believe that it all started with *you!* So, before you turn on the waterworks, and start blaming the rest of the world for the lost time with your son, why don't you do some self-reflection and remember why you lost that time in the first place!"

With that, Carmen left him to reflect on his demons while she moved onto the next self-obsessed moron who didn't deserve to mourn her precious Brian.

Ben.

"What do *you* want?" Carmen growled.

"To pay my respects. I *did* love him once, you know," Ben said, not a single syllable sounding sincere.

"You certainly had a funny way of showing it," Carmen scowled.

"I know! And, believe it or not, I'm not proud of what I did."

"Are you at least going to take some responsibility for what happened?"

"What are you talking about? He was shot? Surely you should be blaming *her* over there! Didn't she hate Brian? And shouldn't *she* have been in charge of the bank security shit, or whatever?" he said pointing towards Susan.

"Oh, you have got to be fucking kidding me! What the hell is *she* doing here?" Carmen raged, making a beeline for Susan. She didn't want to waste any more time on Ben, anyway. He was a narcissist who only cared about looking good, not actually being a decent human being.

"Oi! What are you doing here?"

"I knew *you'd* be here," Susan replied. "You've been avoiding my calls all week."

"Yeah, and for good reason," Carmen rebutted, gesturing at the funeral service around them.

"Yes . . . well . . . I came to tell you that your bereavement leave ends today, so I expect to see you back in work tomorrow," Susan answered coldly.

"Are you fucking *for real*?" Carmen twitched in anger.

"Yes, I'm always 'for real'," the hag answered, using honest-to-god air-quote fingers.

"You know what. On behalf of both me *and* Brian, you can take your job and stick it up your ass!"

"Oh, *do* behave, Carmen," Susan said, as if disciplining a child, not that Susan had a maternal bone in her body.

"Oh, *do* drop dead, you wicked bitch! I quit! Now, get the fuck out of here before they have to start digging another hole!" Carmen said, so furiously that spit flew, hitting Susan's now-horrified face.

Susan left.

As did Brian's father.

And his ex.

"Sorry to take the Lord's name in vain – and at a *funeral*, no less – but, Jesus Christ! Is anyone actually here for *Brian*?" Carmen broke down into tears.

After a few minutes of sobbing, only stopping to throw her handful of dirt onto the coffin, Carmen felt a hand on her shoulder, and a comforting voice sounded behind her.

"Hey, are you alright?" She turned to see a tall, handsome man. "Sorry, that was a stupid question. Of course you're not okay," he added. Seeing her tear-flooded face, the man instinctively just opened up his arms to offer a hug. And, though Carmen didn't know him, she knew that sometimes, a stranger is the easiest person to be vulnerable with, and she buried her head into his chest.

"I'm sorry for your loss," he said.

"Thank you," Carmen pulled away, dabbing her cheek with a tissue. "How did you know Brian?"

"Well, this might sound a bit weird but . . . I didn't. I just started working at this veterinary practice and we always have the news on in the background. When I saw the picture of Brian, and heard the story, I just had this . . . overwhelming feeling that I needed to be here and say goodbye. You picked a great picture. He was a real cutie, huh?"

"He *was* a cutie," Carmen smiled. "You know, you're exactly his type, too. I'm sure he would've *loved* to meet you . . ." she trailed off, prompting him to reveal his name.

"Oh, sorry! I'm Logan."

"I'm sure he would've loved to meet you, *Logan*." Carmen wiped away the tears, allowing a smile to creep out of the corner of her mouth.

TOO LATE?

"Thanks," he smiled. "Oh, what's this?" He looked down to see a small, fluffy, slightly mucky dog. "Well, aren't *you* just adorable," he said, picking the pup up and holding it to his face.

"You should keep her," Carmen suggested.

"Oh, I don't know about that. I've already got a grumpy pug at home called Rex."

"Ah, go on! She looks like she can handle herself," Carmen gave the pup a stroke.

"Yeah, she does, doesn't she? Fine if she hasn't been chipped, I'll take her in. What should I call her?"

"Well, she's pretty lucky to have found you so... how about that? *Lucky*."

"It's a bit cheesy but, yeah! I like it."

"Thank you for being here today, for Brian," Carmen said. "It's nice to see someone not just here to make themselves feel better. I really appreciate it."

"No need to thank me. Like I said, I think I was... supposed... to be here."

"Yeah, me too," she smiled.

The ceremony came to an end, and Logan left with his newfound furry friend, leaving Carmen alone with Brian for the final time. She dropped to her knees on the freshly laid dirt and placed her hand upon it, just to be closer to him.

"Hey, kiddo," she sobbed. "It's really not the same without you, and I know that you probably think I'm just being a drama queen because it's only been a week, but it's true. I miss you so much, and I'm sorry that I wasn't there for you when you needed me. I should've told you just how much I loved you more often. I should've forced you to talk to me. But I didn't, because *I* was too scared. I didn't know how to tackle it, because *I* was the coward. I'm sorry I let you down, and I know it's too late to change anything. But, I promise, I'll do my best to make sure that every other little gay boy in the world feels loved the way you deserved to.

"I hope that you're in a peaceful place now, and that one day, I'll be up there with you, and we can watch *Drag Race: All Stars Season Forty-Six* together. Oh, and I can't *wait* to tell you about the hunk that came to your funeral! I think you guys would've really hit it off!"

"For now, though, goodbye bestie.

MORE FROM THE AUTHOR

If you enjoyed this story, please check out A. W. Jackson's ever-expanding crossover fantasy universe. To find out more about these books, visit: www.awjackson.co.uk.

Madame Voodoo
The Pudding Lane Witch

Madame Voodoo and The Voodoo King Coming Late 2025

Printed in Great Britain
by Amazon